Anna Alice Chapin

Wonder Tales from Wagner

Told for Young People

Anna Alice Chapin

Wonder Tales from Wagner
Told for Young People

ISBN/EAN: 9783337071721

Printed in Europe, USA, Canada, Australia, Japan

Cover: Foto ©Andreas Hilbeck / pixelio.de

More available books at **www.hansebooks.com**

WONDER TALES FROM WAGNER

Told for Young People

BY

ANNA ALICE CHAPIN

AUTHOR OF "THE STORY OF THE RHINEGOLD"

ILLUSTRATED

NEW YORK AND LONDON

HARPER & BROTHERS PUBLISHERS

1898

TO

THE CHILDREN

WHO MAY HEAR

RICHARD WAGNER'S OPERAS

IN THE HOPE OF AIDING THEM TO UNDERSTAND

THOSE MASTERPIECES

THIS BOOK

Is Dedicated

"*Hark! Gay fanfares from halls of old Romance*
Strike through the clouds of clamor: who be these
That, paired in rich processional, advance
From darkness . . . . ?
Bright ladies and brave knights of Fatherland,
Sad mariners no harbor e'er may hold,
A swan soft floating towards a magic strand;
Dim ghosts of earth, air, water, fire, steel, gold,
Wind, grief, and love; a lewd and lurking band
Of Powers—dark Conspiracy, Cunning cold,
Gray Sorcery . . . .
O Wagner, westward bring thy heavenly art,
No trifler thou . . . .

. . . .

Thine ears hear deeper than thine eyes can see."

SIDNEY LANIER.

PREFACE

RICHARD WAGNER, in constructing his music dramas, found his materials in the legends of all lands. The source, or more correctly the sources, of "The Flying Dutchman"—essentially a sea-myth—are to be traced to many countries. "Tannhäuser," the mediæval tale of which has been recorded in poetry, and thus handed down to us from the past, is distinctly German. So, too, is "Lohengrin," though the story of Cupid and Psyche, from which Wagner obtained part of the plot of this opera, is Greek. "Tristan and Isolde" is Celtic; and "The Mastersingers" has an historical foundation, and is peopled with real, not legendary, personages. It is my purpose to show, as simply as I can, the origin of the stories incorporated in the Master's works.

The legend of "The Flying Dutchman" is the most widely known sea-story in existence. It is common to all lands, and sailors to this day tell tales of the strange ship which passes a certain latitude

on a certain night of the year. The captain who
commands her bears many names, though it is gen-
erally believed that the varying tales told in different tongues are but versions of one original legend,
which, probably, was diffused over many lands by
repetitions among the sailors. In the world of literature we often find the unfortunate captain. Cole-
ridge's Ancient Mariner, though from a different
cause, is obliged to

> "Pass like night from land to land;"

and in the description of his vessel, given by the
Hermit in the same poem, we find a strange sem-
blance to the ship of the Flying Dutchman:

> "'Strange, by my faith,' the Hermit said—
> 'And they answered not our cheer!
> The planks look warped! and see those sails,
>   How thin they are and sere!
> I never saw aught like to them,
>   Unless perchance it were
> Brown skeletons of leaves'" . . .

We are reminded of Wagner's "Traft ihr das
Schiff im Meere an?" in the following:

> "But why drives on that ship so fast,
> Without nor wave nor wind?"

It is said that Wagner was influenced in the writing of this opera by the story contained in Heine's

Memoirem des Herrn von Schnabelewopski, and by other writers, Wilhelm Hauff among them. The latter has told his weird tale of the phantom ship *Carmilhan* most effectively, having introduced, instead of a demoniacal chorus, a sad and slow song, sung by the doomed seafarers. The following description of the marching of the uncanny procession down the rocks to their ship, after a short sojourn on land, is to be found in Edward Stowell's translation of Hauff's story : " The whole procession marched away in the same order in which it had come, and with the same solemn song, which grew ever fainter and fainter in the distance, until finally it was lost in the roar of the breakers." The tall and gloomy captain, Alfred Frank von Schwelder, of Amsterdam, is easily identified with Vanderdecken.

Wagner conceived his plan for the construction of " Der Fliegende Holländer " while on his voyage from Pillau to London. He declared afterwards that he had been greatly interested in the tales of the sailors, and their confirmation of that particular legend, and it is probable that in this way a deeper impression was made upon him than by the works already written on the subject. On that voyage, too, he undoubtedly felt and assimilated that wonderful and indescribable soul of the sea which subsequently gave so distinct a coloring to " Der Fliegende Holländer."

Wagner first found the legend of "Tannhäuser" in the verses of Ludwig Tieck. The story is an old one, but has been less frequently the subject of poetry and prose than most of the legends from which Wagner took his plots. The reason for this is probably the extreme difficulty of treating the tale adequately. After that of the Master, the best version which has ever appeared is Owen Meredith's "Battle of the Bards." This poem is most beautiful, and that Meredith's conception of Elizabeth's character is the same as Wagner's is shown in the lines in which he compares her to

> "The pale
> Mild-eyed March violet of the North, that blows
> Bleak under bergs of ice."

The first part of this poem is the description of the coming of the Pope's messenger. Here, too, the poet closely follows Wagner. He says that there came into the valley

> "A flying post, and in his hand he bore
> A wither'd staff o'er flourish'd with green leaves."

He was followed by

> "A crowd of youth and eld
> That sang to stun with sound the lark in heaven,
> 'A miracle! a miracle from Rome!
> Glory to God that makes the bare bough green!'"

Sir Walther von der Vogelweide, the Minnesinger, is the subject of many poems. He was called the Bard of Love, and was wont to declare that he had learned his art of song from the birds. Longfellow, in his " Walter von der Vogelweid," relates how the great master, when dying in the cloister of Wurtz-burg, enjoined the monks to feed the birds every day in his name. This was done according to his behest.

> "On the cross-bar of each window,
>   On the lintel of each door,
> They renewed the War of Wartburg
>   Which the bard had fought before."

At last the portly abbot murmured, " Why this waste of food?" and thereafter the meal was turned to loaves for the brotherhood, and the birds went hungry.

> "But around the vast cathedral,
>   By sweet echoes multiplied,
> Still the birds repeat the legend,
>   And the name of Vogelweid."

Wagner obtained much of his material for the opera of " Lohengrin " from " Parzival "—Wolfram von Eschenbach's epic poem. Lohengrin may have a prototype in Sir Galahad, of whom Tennyson has written such inspired poetry. The characters of the two knights are somewhat similar — the strength,

spirituality, nobility, and great personal courage being equally developed in both. The special differ-
ences between their lives are that Galahad seeks the
Holy Grail, while Lohengrin is one of its recognized
guardians ; that Galahad leaves men, to lead his life
alone, in ceaseless endeavor and in communion with
angelic hosts, while Lohengrin abandons his high
and celestial estate to mingle with humanity and
love a mortal woman. The legend of the Holy
Grail is universally familiar, and, as is well known,
figures importantly in the " Idyls of the King." I
have written of the mystic cup further on, and need
not speak of it here. The plot of "Lohengrin" is
to be found in the legends of Jupiter and Semele,
and of Pururavas and Urvasi, but its most familiar
form is the tale of Cupid and Psyche. In all these
instances curiosity and anxiety prove stronger than
love, a promise is broken, and sorrow ensues.

Of all Celtic legends, that of Tristan, Tristram, or
Tristrem, and Isolde, Iseult, or Isolt, is the most
popular, the most poetical, and the best suited for
use in literature. Among those who have written
of the love and sorrow of the Knight of Lyonesse,
or Lionelle, and the lady whom he loved, are Matthew Arnold, Algernon Swinburne, Alfred Tennyson,
and Sir Walter Scott. Matthew Arnold sings well of

> " Those who lived and loved
> A thousand years ago."

Yet, in spite of its poetical beauty, his version of
the tale seems wanting in the dramatic feeling which
caused Wagner to centre the interest in his two lovers alone, entirely omitting Iseult of Brittany. In
Arnold's poem this second Iseult is so sweet and her
fate is so touching that we lose something of the intensity, and much of the concentration, which thrills
us in Wagner's music drama. The second Iseult
figures also in Swinburne's "Tristram of Lyonesse,"
and is a less attractive and touching character than
Arnold's. Swinburne's poem is exquisite, however.
The beginning seems to express Wagner's prelude
in words, and the last part is replete with beauty.
The King, after the lover's death, builds a chapel by
the ocean ; in that chapel he entombs the two so
well beloved by him. The years pass, and the water
rises and ingulfs the chapel. So over it forever is

"The light and sound and darkness of the sea."

Tennyson's story of Tristram and Isolt is contained in "The Last Tournament," and is unimpor-
tant as a version of the ancient tale. In "Thomas
the Rhymer," by Sir Walter Scott, we find the sim-
plest version of the legend. It is identical with
Wagner's opera, save for the characterization of
Marke as "cowardly." At a feast spread in Ercil-
doune, Thomas the Rhymer sings to the assembly

many songs of chivalry—tales of the Round Table
and of the great knights of ancient times. At last,
in melodious song, he relates the tale of Tristrem,
Knight of Lionelle, who slew Morholde, and bore a
"venom'd wound" for the sake of his uncle, King
Marke of Cornwall. The poem continues as follows:

> "No art the poison could withstand,
>   No medicine could be found,
> Till lovely Isolde's lily hand
>   Had probed the rankling wound.

> "With gentle hand and soothing tongue
>   She bore the leech's part;
> And, while she o'er his sick-bed hung,
>   He paid her with his heart.

> "Oh, fatal was the gift, I ween!
>   For, doomed in evil tide,
> The maid must be rude Cornwall's queen,
>   His cowardly uncle's bride.
>   .   .   .   .

> "Through many a maze the winning song
>   In changeful passion led,
> Till bent at last the listening throng
>   O'er Tristrem's dying bed.

> "His ancient wounds their scars expand,
>   With agony his heart is wrung:
> Oh, where is Isolde's lily hand,
>   And where her soothing tongue?

"She comes! she comes!—like flash of flame
 Can lovers' footsteps fly ;
 She comes! she comes!—she only came
 To see her Tristrem die.
 .   .   .   .
 "There paused the harp; its lingering sound
 Died slowly on the ear ;
 The silent guests still bent around,
 For still they seemed to hear."

The Mastersingers of Nuremberg were undoubtedly as authentic as other historical persons, and the
twelve good men of the famous guild left behind
them stable proofs that they had lived. There are
poems in existence to-day signed by Sixtus Beckmesser, Veit Pogner, and the other masters. Hans
Sachs's mastersongs are looked upon with reverence
nowadays, and his name, with that of Albrecht
Dürer, is invariably mentioned in connection with
Nuremberg.

"Thy songs, Hans Sachs, are living yet,
 In honest, hearty German,"

says Whittier, and we find innumerable references
to the cobbler-poet in both poetry and prose. If
the poem " Walter von der Vogelweid " be read in
connection with " The Mastersingers of Nuremberg,"
new light will be thrown by the legend of the birds
upon Walther von Stolzing's declaration that " in
the woods he learned his singing." The feathered

minstrels which had taught song to the gentle Bard of Love, and which still sang the record of his kindliness and tender thought, taught also the knight who in their voices found the music which best expressed the emotions of his own heart.

The Mastersingers have attracted more than one writer, but of all attempts at capturing the spirit of the old art-loving burghers the best is Longfellow's " Nuremberg," in which the very soul of Wagner's work seems manifest :

" In the valley of the Pegnitz, where across broad meadow-
    lands
Rise the blue Franconian mountains, Nuremberg the an-
    cient stands.

" Quaint old town of toil and traffic, quaint old town of
    art and song,
Memories haunt thy pointed gables like the rooks that
    round them throng.

" Memories of the Middle Ages, when the emperors, rough
    and bold,
Had their dwelling in thy castle, time-defying, centuries
    old.

" And thy brave and thrifty burghers boasted in their un-
    couth rhyme,
That their great imperial city stretched its hand through
    every clime.

"Through these streets so broad and stately, these obscure
and dismal lanes,
Walked of yore the Mastersingers, chanting rude poetic
strains.

"From remote and sunless suburbs came they to the
friendly guild,
Building nests in Fame's great temple, as in spouts the
swallows build.

"As the weaver plied his shuttle, wove he too the mystic
rhyme,
And the smith his iron measures hammered to the an-
vil's chime;

"Thanking God, whose boundless wisdom makes the flowers of poesy bloom
In the forge's dust and cinders, in the tissues of the
loom.

"Here Hans Sachs, the cobbler-poet, laureate of the gentle craft,
Wisest of the Twelve Wise Masters, in huge folios sang
and laughed.

. . . .

"Vanished is the ancient splendor, and before my dreamy
eye
Wave these mingled shapes and figures, like a faded tap-
estry.

"Not thy Councils, not thy Kaisers, win for these the
world's regard,
But thy painter, Albrecht Dürer, and Hans Sachs, thy cob-
bler-bard."

CONTENTS

THE FLYING DUTCHMAN
(*Der Fliegende Holländer*)

TANNHÄUSER

LOHENGRIN

TRISTAN AND ISOLDE
(*Tristan und Isolde*)

THE MASTERSINGERS OF NUREMBERG
(*Die Meistersinger*)

ILLUSTRATIONS

THE FLYING DUTCHMAN

(Der Fliegende Holländer)

CHAPTER I

THE SPELLBOUND SEAMAN

SAILORS believe that there is an Evil Spirit of the ocean who, like the ancient Sea - Queen Ran, "would many a man beguile," and who delights in casting spells upon unfortunate mortals and in dragging them down under the waves. He has terrible power, they declare, and can arouse the ocean to wrath, collect the thunder-clouds, and let loose the wild storm-winds—indeed, the number of vessels he has wrecked cannot be counted. His mighty magic enables him to doom mariners to fearful fates if they displease or defy him; and of this magic you shall now hear.

There was once a Dutch sea-captain named Van-derdecken, who, after a long and prosperous voyage, directed his course towards his home in Holland. He was a brave-hearted but rash man, and, on hearing of a certain particularly dangerous cape, called Good Hope, he vowed that he would double that cape, come what might, if it took all eternity.

Now the Sea-Spirit heard this vow, and laughed
—for he loved well to punish men for defying his
power — and wove spells about the ship, the captain, and the crew. From that day enchantment
lay upon them, and they were doomed to traverse
the seas forever—trying always to sail around the
Cape of Good Hope, and failing at every trial.
Long years passed, and Vanderdecken and his crew
were only kept from death by the Sea-Spirit, who
condemned them to sail forever.

The unfortunate seaman had but one hope of
happiness and salvation: if a woman would give
him her love, and remain faithful to him until death,
the spell would be lifted and Vanderdecken freed.
Every seven years he was allowed to cast anchor
and go on shore to search for the woman who
would save him through her love and fidelity.
But, alas! he could find none, and as the end of
every term on land expired, bringing the return
of the fateful spell, the Dutchman put to sea for
seven more long years.

Time passed, and still he wandered over the
ocean in his ship, which seemed winged, so fast was
her flight. Still, the sight of her hull startled passing mariners, for a wierd light glimmered about it,
her sails were red as blood, and her masts as black
as the black depths of the night. Thus had she
been changed by the Sea-Spirit, to show that his

spell was about her and all on board. Every one who saw the ship felt a sense of mystery creep over him, and regarded her passing, at the commencement of a voyage, as no auspicious sign.

Sometimes a glimpse of a pale face at the prow filled all hearts with terror and pity, for every one knew that it was the spellbound Seaman who gazed out to sea as though seeking the help which never came.

Every sailor knew Vanderdecken's story and the power which doomed him to eternally sail the seas, and they had given him a name descriptive of his wanderings. When, with all sails set and the waves rushing past her sides, his ship flew by in the wind, seafarers changed their course, and whispered, fearfully, "Yonder sails the Flying Dutchman!"

Once upon a time there lived a Norwegian captain named Daland. He made many long voyages, none of them very prosperous, and, consequently, he had a great love for gold. He was not a bad man, but he was foolish enough to worship and envy all those in possession of greater wealth than himself. While he sailed away in search of riches, he used to leave his daughter in the care of her old nurse.

The day on which the story opens he had returned from a long voyage, and had met a severe storm, in which he had put to shore on a part of the Norwegian coast which he recognized as Sand-wike Bay, forty miles from his own port. The wind had fallen, and, as his crew were tired, he ordered them to rest. He directed the steersman to keep watch while the others slept; but the man, being drowsy himself, soon fell asleep at his post, after singing a song to the south wind, beseeching it to rise and blow him to his Norwegian sweetheart.

At the moment when his eyes closed a ship appeared on the sea speeding towards the shore. As she came the storm rose again, with violent mutterings, increasing in rage. The sky darkened rapidly, and the sea was lashed into fury by the whips of the wind. The ship approached swiftly, and the anchor crashed through the water. Noiselessly the crew furled the blood-red sails and coiled the ropes. With the uncertain step of one who had not set foot on solid earth for years, the captain of the ship went on shore. His face was ghastly pale, his hair and beard were long and black, in his eyes was an indescribable yearning. It was Vanderdecken, the Flying Dutchman.

As he stood on the rock-strewn shore he thought of his seven years' flight over the seas, of the sadness of his doom, and the hopelessness of his quest. At last he broke into passionate words, saying that he longed only for the end of the universe, when the sea, and he with it, would be gone. And in the hold of the ship his sailors, under the same strange spell, echoed his words in hollow tones.

He had relapsed into silence and stood leaning against a rock, wrapped in gloomy thought, when Daland came out from the cabin of his ship. Seeing the vessel at anchor near by, he hastily aroused his sleeping steersman, upbraiding him for his negligence and pointing out the strange ship. Once awake, the steersman seized the speaking-trumpet and shouted, " Ahoy !"

Only the echoes answered.

Suddenly Daland perceived Vanderdecken on the shore, and, advancing to the ship's side, cried aloud, " Hallo, seaman ! What name have you, and what country ?"

There was a long silence. Then, without moving, the Dutchman answered, slowly, " I have come from afar. Would you drive me from anchorage ?"

" Heaven forbid !" said Daland, warmly. " I give you welcome, seaman."

He left the ship, and, joining the Dutchman on the rocks, asked, with friendly interest, " Who are you ?"

" A Dutchman," was Vanderdecken's sole reply.

" Good greeting !" said Daland. " I suppose you were brought by the storm to this bare, rocky strand ? I am in that same plight ; but my home is not far away, and I shall soon reach it. Whence have you come? Have you weathered the storm well?"

"My ship is strong," returned the Dutchman. "It weathers all storms."

Then, speaking in accents fraught with deep sadness, he said that he had long sailed the seas, and that for certain melancholy reasons he could never return to his native land. He ended by beseeching Daland to give him shelter in his house for the night, saying that he would repay his kindness with riches brought from every land. To give force to his words, he motioned to two of his sailors on board the ship, who raised a large chest between them and carried it on shore.

"Now you will see many treasures," said the Dutchman, raising the lid. "Behold, and convince yourself that they are of great value."

Daland was fairly dazzled at the wonders revealed to his gaze; costly pearls, incomparable gems of all sorts, they formed a spectacle absolutely astounding to the simple sea-captain. As the Dutchman went on to declare, sadly, that the stones were useless to him, who had neither wife nor child, and to offer them freely for a single night's rest and shelter, Daland could scarcely believe that he heard aright.

Vanderdecken continued to talk with him, and on discovering that he had a daughter, asked permission to woo her. Though somewhat startled at this sudden request, Daland could not forget the glitter of the jewels, which proved the stranger's great wealth; moreover, he had descried in all that he had said a melancholy grandeur which seemed to indicate nobility of soul. After a few doubtful words, Daland gave his consent to the Dutchman's suit, speaking tenderly of the unceasing gentleness and devoted love of the daughter whom he was relinquishing.

"So she will be mine!" murmured Vanderdecken, musingly. "Will *she* be my angel of rescue?"

The storm had blown over, and the wind had changed. It now blew freshly from the south, and the steersman sang gayly a few bars of his song in greeting. The sailors, waving their caps, shouted, "Hoho! Haloho!"

"The wind is fair," said Daland. "The sea is calm, so let us weigh anchor and set sail for home."

Well knowing that his ship, when under weigh, bore a strange and uncanny appearance, which none could fail to recognize, the Dutchman begged leave to wait and follow later in the day, giving as a reason for his request his crew's fatigue and need of rest.

Daland, with a cheery farewell, went on board his own ship and blew a signal on his whistle. The sailors set the sails, singing joyfully; the anchor was weighed, and the vessel left the bay.

The Dutchman then boarded his ship in silence.

CHAPTER II

IN THE HOUSE OF DALAND

ON the afternoon of the same day a number of maidens went to pay a visit to Daland's daughter, Senta, and her old nurse, Dame Mary. As was the custom among neighbors, they brought their spinning-wheels, and soon installed themselves in the living-room, chatting, spinning, and singing.

Daland's house was rude and rough, but comparatively well furnished, and the room in which the young girls sat was large and cheerful. There was a broad fireplace, and because of the cold air of Norway, all had drawn their chairs close to the bright blaze. On the walls hung various paintings and rude prints of sea subjects, and several ocean charts. At one side of the room was a large portrait of a man in black Spanish dress; near it stood a deep arm-chair, in which Senta sat.

A very beautiful maiden was the daughter of Daland. Her gray eyes were large and dreamy, her

"THE SAILORS, WAVING THEIR CAPS, SHOUTED 'HOHO! HALOHO!'"

soft hair pale gold, her coloring most delicate and clear, and a look of intensity, of suppressed emotion, and, above all, of unfulfilled longing, lent a strange and passionate sadness to her face. She sat in abstracted meditation, with her eyes fixed on the pale face of the man in the portrait. It was that of the Flying Dutchman, painted long years ago, and had fallen into Daland's possession in the course of his travels. Old Mary had often sung to the girl the ballad which told the history of the original of the picture, and the sad tale had made a deep impression upon Senta's sensitive nature. She spent much of her time musing beside the portrait and dreaming of the doomed mariner, the spellbound Flying Dutchman.

The maidens spun on, chatting with old Dame Mary, who sat by her wheel, urging them to swifter work, the bright firelight flickering over her kindly wrinkled face and quaint Norwegian dress. The girls, interrupting themselves with laughter and merry jests, sang a harmonious spinning song as the wheels hummed and the fire crackled in accompaniment.

"Why are you silent, Senta?" asked Mary, with some impatience. "You lazy child, will you not spin? See her there," she added, turning to the laughing maidens, "still before that portrait!" With growing anxiety she again addressed Senta:

" Why will you so gaze, all your young life, dreaming before that picture!"

" Why have you told me the story of his griefs?"
said Senta, sitting motionless. " Oh, the unhappy
man!" she added, more softly.

" What did she say?" asked the maidens of Dame
Mary. " Is she sighing for that pale man? That is
why she looks so wan."

" Senta, turn and join us," begged Mary.

" She does not hear you," said the maidens, and
one or two broke out, jestingly, " She's in love!
She's in love! It is to be hoped Erik will not be
angry; he has a quick temper, and you would better
say nothing, for he might fall into a rage and shoot
his rival—off the wall!"

They all laughed at this sally, and it was some
time before their merriment subsided. Senta sprang
to her feet in evident displeasure. " Oh, silence
your foolish laughter!" she exclaimed. " Are you
trying to anger me?" The girls began to sing loudly
so as to drown her voice, and turned their wheels
with a great clatter.

" Make an end to this stupid song!" besought
Senta, almost wild from the continued noise. " If
you would win me to your way, let me hear something better than that."

" Good!" cried the maidens. " Sing, then, yourself!"

"I would rather hear Dame Mary," said Senta, turning to her old nurse. "If she will sing us the Ballad."

"I will not!" declared Mary. "Let the Flying Dutchman rest."

"Then I will sing it myself," announced Senta, with suppressed excitement. "Listen, and mark the words."

"We will rest and stop spinning," cried the girls, and, springing up, they put away their wheels, then drew their chairs close to Senta, and prepared to listen. Mary, angered by the girl's persistence in harping on a dreary and useless subject, remained by the fire and continued to spin.

Sitting in the arm-chair, Senta gazed steadily on the portrait before her, and gave the sailors' call: "Yohohoe! Yohohoe! Yohohoe!" Then in clear, thrilling tones, now powerful, now soft, she sang the Ballad of the Flying Dutchman:

"See you the ship upon the sea,
    With blood-red sails and masts of black?
    On board her captain—pale is he!—
    Holds restless watch through tempests' wrack.
        Hui! How sobs the wind!
            Yohohoe!
        Pipes in cordage twined!
            Yohohoe!
Hui! Like an arrow flies he, without end, without hope,
    without rest!

"Yet can this pallid man from his endless spell be set
    free,
Finds he a woman true, who at death still faithful will be.
Oh, when mayst thou, lonely Mariner, find her?
Pray ye that Heaven may one soon send, true to the
    end."

As she sang the last words Senta gazed with increased intensity at the picture. The maidens,
much interested, leaned forward, forgetting to chat-
ter or laugh. Mary, absorbed in spite of herself in
the oft-told tale, had ceased to spin, and sat listening in the dying firelight.

"Once through fierce wind and tempest loud,
    To sail around a cape wished he,
And to succeed he rashly vowed,
    'Though it might take eternity!'
        Hui! The Sea-Sprite heard!
            Yohohoe!
        Hui! He took his word!
            Yohohoe!
Hui! And enslaved he now sails on the sea, without rest,
    without end!

"Yet can the mournful man be set free from earthly
    spell,
Would but an angel stoop, and the way to his salvation
    tell!
Ah, mightest thou, lonely Mariner, find her!
Pray ye that Heaven may one soon send, true to the
    end."

Senta had risen to her feet, and now sang, with strong and overwhelming passion, the last verse of the ballad :

"He anchors every seven years ;
     To seek a wife he goes on land;
He seeks through all the seven years,
     But no true woman gives her hand.
          Hui ! Set sails ! away !
               Yohohoe !
          Hui ! The anchor weigh !
               Yohohoe !
Hui ! Falsest love — falsest truth ! Off to sea, without rest, without end !"

With the last words Senta sank into the chair, exhausted, and there was a deep silence.

"Ah, where is God's angel who will guide him?" whispered the maidens, softly. "Where is she who will remain true until death?"

A look of wild exaltation shone in Senta's face, her eyes sought the portrait.

"Through me—through me you shall be saved!" she cried.

"Senta!" exclaimed Dame Mary, anxiously. "Senta! Senta!" cried the maidens in chorus. They sprang from their seats, and drew back, terrified, believing her to be mad.

"Senta," said a sorrowful voice at the door, "will you so hurt me?"

The girls, hearing the words, turned, crying, "Help us, Erik! Help! She is distraught!"

Erik entered slowly, as though dazed with grief. He was a young huntsman, well-beloved in the neighborhood, and though poor, always generous with such gifts as were in his power to bestow— game shot by his own hand on the hills or in the woods. A handsome, impetuous, and hot-blooded young hunter was Erik, and Senta's tender and devoted lover. Upon leaving home for his long voyage, Daland had placed his daughter under Erik's protection, satisfied that between him and good Dame Mary she would be well cared for, and as closely sheltered from every misfortune as if he himself were at home. Senta had always been fond of Erik, but had never returned the deep love which he felt for her. Of late she had seemed brooding and dreamy; nevertheless the shock from her words, which he had overheard, was no less keen because it was not wholly unexpected. As he came into the room his handsome face was pale, and despair was evident in every line of his naturally erect and lithe figure.

Dame Mary, with an expression of mingled sorrow and fear upon her face, stood looking at Senta, who still sat in the arm-chair, seeming blind to her surroundings and with a look of dreamy ecstasy in her eyes.

" My very blood grows cold," said the old nurse, trembling and sighing. Then, with a rising note of anger in her voice, she added, " Horrible picture, you will soon go when her father returns !"

" Her father is now coming," said Erik, advancing. His voice was full of pain ; his eyes sought those of Senta.

" My father comes?" she cried, springing from the chair as though but just awakened.

" From the rocks I saw his ship draw near," returned Erik.

At this the maidens, greatly excited, prepared to run to the shore to meet the ship; but Dame Mary's chiding voice reminded them of household duties left undone, all of which must be completed before they could greet the sailors. They all left the room, Dame Mary following them, like a bird driving her brood before her.

The door closed, and Erik was alone with Senta. She wished to hasten to meet her father, but Erik passionately besought her to remain and give him some explanation of her strange behavior. Senta endeavored to soothe him by declaring that she naturally felt pity for the sorrowful man in the picture, and asked him, half-laughingly, if he were really afraid of a song and a face.

" Should not a pitiable fate touch my heart?" she questioned, gently.

2

"My sorrow touches you not," answered Erik, gloomily.

"What can your sorrow be compared to his!" she exclaimed, drawing him before the picture. Indicating the pain with which he seemed to look down from the canvas, she spoke sadly and compassionately of the misery of his doom. "When I remember that he never finds rest," she said, softly, "what great woe stirs in my heart!"

"Alas!" said Erik, in tones of deep and tragic meaning, "I think of a dream which lately came to me." He shuddered.

"What terrifies you so greatly?" asked Senta, startled by his expression of horror.

"Senta," he said, in a low voice, "listen, and heed the warning!"

Senta sank into the arm-chair, and her eyes closed; she seemed to be in a trance, through the mists of which she still heard Erik's voice distinctly.

"On the cliffs I lay dreaming," he began, leaning on the chair in which she sat. "I saw under me the waters of the ocean. I heard the surf as it rushed, shining, to break on the strand. I perceived a strange ship near the shore—weird and wonderful it seemed. Next I saw two men approaching—one I knew; it was your father."

"The other?" muttered Senta, with closed eyes.

" Well I knew him, too. In blackest garb, with palest mien—he it was—the Seaman!" He pointed to the portrait.

" And I?" murmured Senta.

" You flew to greet your father. I saw you kneel at the feet of the stranger—"

" He raised me up—" whispered Senta, with dreamy excitement.

" In his arms," said Erik, his voice growing tremulous with suppressed passion. " I saw him clasp you in deep happiness."

" And then?" cried Senta, softly.

Erik gazed at her wonderingly and anxiously. His voice dropped to a low and sorrowful key: " I saw you put to sea together."

Senta opened her eyes; they were blazing with excitement and exultation.

" He searches for me!" she cried. " I must wait for him! With him I will go to death!"

" Alas!" gasped Erik, despairingly. " My dream told truth!"

He rushed from the house in wild grief and sorrow. Senta remained seated in the chair, humming the refrain from the ballad:

" Ah, mightest thou, lonely Mariner, find her!
Pray ye that Heaven may one soon send, true to the—"

The door opened, and two men entered. One,

her father, she hardly noticed; but the face of the other forced a cry from her lips. She looked swiftly from the pictured face to that of the man before her. There was a silence.

" My child," said Daland, coming forward, " have you no greeting for me?"

" Welcome," said Senta, clasping his hand in hers. " My father, say," she added, in a low voice, "who is the stranger?"

Daland explained that his companion was a sailor, like himself, that he possessed great wealth, and that, being far from his own home, he desired shelter in theirs for a short time. He then proceeded to tell her of the Dutchman's desire—that she should be his wife; and, to enforce the proposal, the foolish old captain showed her some jewels, declaring that they were toys compared to the treasures which would be hers when she should wed the rich stranger.

Neither Senta nor the Dutchman spoke, but stood motionless, gazing into each other's faces, as though both were under enchantment. Daland, slightly disappointed at their apparent indifference, whispered to his daughter that she must not discard such an exceptional opportunity, and left them alone together.

In the pause which followed Vanderdecken remembered his fruitless quest, and asked himself if

it could be true that this maiden would be his angel
of deliverance, and Senta tried to realize this sudden and overwhelming happiness—that it was indeed she who was the woman who would save
him.

Then the Dutchman slowly approached her. He
asked her if she would abide by her father's choice
and accept him as her husband—if she would remain true to him until death.

"Whoever you are," said Senta, solemnly, "wherever you may go, whatever is the fate which you
and I must meet together, I am ready to abide by
my father's choice."

"Alas!" said the Mariner. "If you knew who I
was you would fear to give up all things for me
and bid me trust you."

There was a light in Senta's face as she
answered, "I know what truth is — my heart
shows me the right. I will be faithful until
death."

A few moments later Daland entered boisterously, and being satisfied that the stranger's wooing
had prospered, asked leave to give his people a
feast in honor of the betrothal. He declared that
some sort of merrymaking was expected at the end
of every voyage, and assured the Dutchman and
Senta that one and all would rejoice with them in
their happiness.

"To the feast!" he cried, joyfully, and led them out to join in the festivities.

The Ballad of the Flying Dutchman

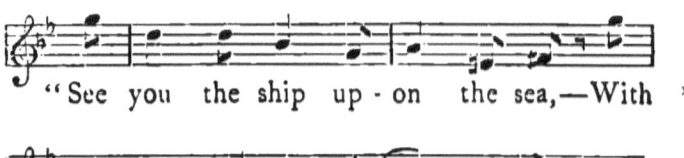

"See you the ship up - on the sea,—With

blood - red sails and masts of black?"

Chorus of Norwegian Sailors

Chorus of the Crew of the Dutch Ship

CHAPTER III

SENTA'S SACRIFICE

THE night fell, cool and clear; there was no sign of wind—the ocean was calm, and the sky cloudless. The two ships were at anchor side by side in a rock-edged bay near Daland's home. Upon his ship the sailors were making merry, and rejoicing at the end of their weary voyage, but the Dutchman's vessel was wrapped in a silence deep as death.

Daland's seamen had lighted their ship brilliantly, and sat singing upon the deck. When they had ended their song they sprang up and danced boisterously, emphasizing the measure with loud stamps. As they danced the merry Norwegian maidens came down over the rocks to the bay, carrying great baskets of food and wine.

"Just look," they said. "They dance! Of course, they want not maidens!" And, pretending to be

offended, they carried their baskets to the Dutch
ship, and called up from the shore, "Hey, sailors!
Hey!" No answer came to them.

"How strange!" they exclaimed, and the Norwegian seamen broke into derisive laughter: "Ha!
ha! Wake them not up! They are asleep!"

"Hey, sailors, answer!" called the maidens.

There was a long, deep silence. Something of the
mystical terror invariably aroused by the ship crept
over maidens and men, though they knew not the
cause.

"Hey, sailors!" called the young girls, still before the Dutch vessel, "will you not come to our
feast?"

"They lie like dragons guarding treasure," said
the Norwegian seamen, laughing.

"Hey, sailors! will you not have wine?" cried the
maidens; and the Norwegians returned, mockingly,
"They drink not! They sing not! and in their ship
they burn no light."

"Have you then no sweethearts on land? Will
you not come and dance with us?"

"They are very old," declared the Norwegians.
"Their hair is white, and their sweethearts are
gone!"

Then one and all cried loudly, "Waken, sailors,
waken!"

In the silence that followed, the strange horror

again made them shudder. The maidens drew back, frightened, and murmured:

"They must be ghosts—food and drink they do not seem to need!"

The Norwegian sailors began to call across to the unseen crew of the Dutch ship.

"Do you know the Flying Dutchman?" they cried, jokingly. "Your ship looks like his!"

"Ah, do not wake them up!" entreated the girls. "They are phantoms—we are sure of it!"

"Maidens, give us some of that food," cried the sailors. "If they are ghosts, we are not, and we should much enjoy your dainties."

"Very well, since your neighbors refuse them," said the girls, and handed up the baskets, which the sailors received with delight. On opening them they cried out at the amount of food and drink within. "Take all you like," laughed the maidens, still somewhat nervous, "but let your tired neighbors rest!" And they hastened away.

"Good friends!" called the sailors, "wake up and join us!"

Through the dim light they fancied that they could see indistinct figures moving on board the Dutch ship.

"Wake up!" repeated the Norwegians. "Wake up! Hussa!"

They drank deeply, and flung their cups to the

deck with a loud noise. The steersman stood
apart, on watch, but joined in the merrymaking.
The sailors finally burst out into a loud drinking-
song:

> "Steersman! Leave the watch!
> Steersman! Come to us!
> Now the sails are rolled,
> Anchor fast,
> Steersman come!

> "Watched we many nights in fearful wind,
> Drank we many times the sea's salt wave,
> Now on watch, we feast and revel find,
> Best of wine to drink the maidens gave!

> "Steersman! Leave the watch!
> Hussa! Hussa!
> Ho! Come and drink with us!"

As they finished singing they noticed that waves
had begun to rise and strike the side of the Dutch
ship. Everywhere else the water was calm, but a
miniature storm seemed to rage around the vessel. A dim blue light played about her prow,
and the weird flames of a ghostly watch-fire flick-
ered on her deck. A shrill wind shrieked in the
rigging, and, as the watch-fire flared up, wild voices
were heard echoing through the darkness, singing
drearily:

"Yohohoe! Yohohoe! Yohohoe!
Ho! Ho! Huissa!
Near to land drives the storm,
Sails are in,
Anchor cast!
Huissa! Run we into the bay!"

The wind in the cordage howled wildly as the
harsh chorus took a definite form.

"Swarthy Master, go on land!
Seven years you sailing flew;
Seek now some fair maiden's hand,
Maiden fair to him be true!

"Gayly now, hui!
Bridegroom! Hui!
Storm winds your Bridal Song,
Ocean to dance to it!
Hui! He pipes!
Captain, ho! are you there?

"Hui! All sails up!
And your bride—say—where stays she?
Hui! Off to sea!
Captain, ho! Captain, ho!
Little love-luck, you see!

"Riot, storm-winds, howl and wail!
Idle rest has not our sail!
Canvas magic-made have we,
Lasting through eternity!
Hoho!
Eternity!"

The ship was tossed up and down as though by unseen hands; the wind sobbed and shrieked ceaselessly between the masts.

The Norwegians, thoroughly frightened, still tried to keep up their courage by continuing their song; but the wild "Hui!" of the Dutch sailors soon made itself heard through their singing, and they relapsed into terror-stricken silence.

The fearful chorus, with its short, shrill exclamations and abrupt changes, continued, increasing in violence, until the Norwegians, fairly overcome with horror, hastily left the deck of the ship, making the sign of the cross to dispel evil magic.

At this wild shouts of laughter were heard from the Dutch crew, and suddenly the waves sank, the blue light vanished, and the same deathlike stillness reigned over the ship, which but a few moments before had been a spectacle of weird and appalling grandeur. The silence was deep, the darkness dense and mysterious. Not a breath of wind stirred the black, calm sea.

Suddenly the door of Daland's house opened, and Senta came out, followed by Erik, who had sought an interview in which to plead with her once more. He could scarcely believe that the news which had been told him could be true—that she was to wed the gloomy stranger of his dream. He besought her passionately to consider well what she did, and spoke of the utter despair which wrung his heart at being so quickly forgotten by her.

He reminded her of the days in which she had at least seemed to love him; when they had wandered in the green valley, and he had climbed gladly to pluck her some highland flowers which she coveted; when her father left them with their hands clasped, bidding him protect her; when they stood together on the high rocks and watched the white glimmer of Daland's departing sail on the far horizon line. He asked her if she had loved him at none of those times. His conviction was evident that she had plighted him her troth and had given him her heart.

At this belief, which wounded him so deeply now that he felt her love was gone, Senta showed herself to be frankly surprised. She assured him that she had never intentionally even seemed to care for him, and endeavored to comfort him, with great patience and sadness. But Erik was deaf to all reason or explanation.

" I believed you true," he said, sorrowfully.

She had no opportunity to answer him, for, with a terrible cry of " Lost! Lost!" the Dutchman rushed past them with a look of deep and tragic despair upon his face. He had overheard the young man's last words, and therefore believed that Senta had been false to Erik, and would, consequently, be false to him. "Hope is eternally lost!" he cried, advancing towards his ship.

"What can this mean!" exclaimed Erik, in astonishment.

"Farewell, Senta!" said the Dutchman, gravely; and though she sprang forward, passionately beseeching him to stay, he only exclaimed, "To sea! To sea! Forget your promise! Forget my salvation! Farewell!"

He blew a long call on his signal-pipe, and cried, "Set sails! Anchor up! Say farewell to the land forever!"

His crew proceeded to get the ship in readiness for departure. Senta endeavored, frantically, to convince him of her constancy, but he would not listen. At last, turning to her, he told her that he was condemned to a terrible fate, which could only be lightened by a true woman's sacrifice. He could not trust her, he said; and his doom decreed that all who should be false to him, after the final vows, would be obliged, like him, to remain under an evil spell forever. From this fate he saved her by relinquishing her as soon as he distrusted her, even vaguely, and before she could regret her determination to be his, or break her promise to be true.

"I know you well," declared Senta; "I know your doom—I knew you when I saw you first. The end of your spell is near—for I am true. You shall find your salvation!"

"Help!" cried Erik, turning first towards the house and then towards the Norwegian ship.

Dame Mary, Daland, the maidens, and the sailors appeared in amazement that changed to horror when they understood the condition of affairs. Poor Daland was especially bewildered and distressed, and Dame Mary was heart-broken, and hurried to her charge with gestures of grief.

The Dutchman turned to Senta. His crew were hoisting the sails and moving about the ship with strange swiftness and silence.

"You know me not," said Vanderdecken, slowly. "But ask the seas of all zones, ask all mariners who have sailed on the seas—they know my ship, whose passing terrifies all gentle hearts. The Flying Dutchman I am called."

The blood-red sails were set, and glowed mysteriously through the darkness. The Dutchman swiftly boarded the ship. It rocked and swayed on the waves, which had now begun to rise. Senta endeavored, wildly, to follow him, but Daland, Erik, and Mary restrained her.

"Yohohoe! Yohohoe! Yohohoe!" shouted the Flying Dutchman's crew, as the ship left shore with the speed of an arrow. "Hoe! Hoe! Hoe!" came the hoarse, weird voices through the dusk. "Huissa!"

" Senta ! Senta !" cried every one, in fear, as she violently freed herself and darted to a high cliff overlooking the sea. "Senta ! What is it you would do?"

" Praise ye the divine will!" she called, with all the power of her passionate soul in her voice, and the words floated out over the waves to the departing ship. " Here stand I, true till death !"

She flung herself into the now seething waters. The surges rolled higher and higher with fierce anger, making huge black walls on either side of the enchanted ship. Then, with a great roar, the water fell upon it, swallowing it from view. The waves whirled wildly over the place where the vessel had sunk, then gradually decreased in violence. The bare masts of the wreck could be seen on the surface of the foaming water.

Then to the watchers a marvellous sight was revealed: as the darkness was dispelled, and in the eastern sky the light of sunrise glowed, they saw the figures of Vanderdecken and Senta floating upward together in the radiance. For the spell had been lifted—the Flying Dutchman was saved.

Motif of Senta's Sacrifice

"' HERE I STAND, TRUE TILL DEATH '"

TANNHÄUSER

Motif of Venus

Song of the Sirens

CHAPTER I

IN THE VENUSBERG

WHEN Christianity became accepted throughout the world, the gods and goddesses were divested of their divinity and relegated to the heart of the earth, where some of them were still worshipped by many people. Among these was Venus, the mighty goddess of Love.

When she was sent from the sunshine and the flowers of the upper world, Venus's heart grew hard. She could not endure the loss of all her power, and as she no longer possessed divine might, she summoned magic to her aid. She became known as a beautiful but wicked sorceress, whose dwelling was a mysterious grotto in a mountain called the Venusberg, situated in the German valley of Thuringia. To this grotto she lured unwatchful mortals, causing them to forget their homes and friends; and they dwelt there, shut away from the upper earth's fresh beauty, in a dim under-world peopled with spirits and sirens and bacchantes—a world full of misty lakes and rose-tinted clouds, and strange lights that came from neither sun nor moon nor stars.

The Venusberg overlooked a broad and fertile valley, where the winds blew freely, where shepherds watched their flocks on the long green slopes, and through which hunting parties often passed on their way to the castle. This castle, which was named the Wartburg, was built on the side of the valley farthest from the Venusberg, and was very large and majestic. In it dwelt the Landgrave Hermann, with his knights and men-at-arms, and his niece, the Princess Elizabeth, with her court ladies. In those days the most cultivated people of the world took a deep interest in the Minnesinger,*

* *Minnesinger:* composed of the German words *Minne,* love, and *Singer,* singers. Literally, then, singers of love.

or minstrels; and the Wartburg was the scene of constant lyrical and musical contests between the bards.

Minstrelsy attracted many knights and nobles so greatly that they learned the art themselves, and in trials of voice, skill, and invention the Minstrel Knights often proved that they well understood the craft of song. One of the best harpers and sweetest singers of Thuringia was a young knight, by name Tannhäuser. He was a favorite at the court of the Landgrave, and, indeed, it was said that the stirring strains which he evoked from his harpstrings, and the wonderful melody of the songs that he sang, had won the love of the proud and beautiful Princess Elizabeth.

The knight, however, in spite of his beloved music, his good friends among the other Minstrel Knights, the kindness of the Landgrave, and the love and admiration which, like so many of the Thuringian nobles, he felt for the Princess, was not happy. He was sad and dreamy, and dissatisfied with his life. He wanted some new and strange experience.

In this spirit he passed one day near the invisible portals of that grotto where so many had entered, but whence none had ever returned. And the enchantress, smiling, put forth her spells and drew him towards her.

As he walked moodily on, his harp in his hand,
his mind busy, as usual, he suddenly raised his eyes,
and, behold, a new and beautiful country was before
him, seen as through a doorway. Countless figures
flitted through the gleaming, ever-changeful rose-
color of the mist that filled the enchanted grotto.
Huge heavy-headed flowers, of strange and lovely
colors, hung in clusters, sending their perfume out
to meet him. Far away he saw the misty waters of
a magical blue lake. The sound of music came to
him, so marvellously, strangely sweet, that to hear it
was almost pain. In the midst of it all was a woman, wondrously beautiful in the rosy light, bending
towards him with beckoning hand. Obeying the
spells which were drawing him with such terrible
power, he passed into the grotto, and could almost
have fancied that a heavy door clanged behind him
as he went.

He stayed in the mystic grotto for a long year,
and thought that he was happy. He watched the
sports of the bacchantes and the nymphs, the mimic
battles, and wild, graceful dances; he listened to the
sweet, chording voices of the sirens; he inhaled the
rich, strong scent of the flowers, and watched the
dissolving mist-wreaths of glowing rose until he
grew almost dizzy. He sat at Venus's feet, and she
taught him songs such as he had never heard before, and wove her spells about him more and more

densely. He gazed at her beautiful face; but the magic veil before him prevented him from seeing the cruel soul which looked out of her eyes, and he worshipped her as the world had worshipped her of old, when she was a grand and noble goddess, who gave the gift of true love to humanity.

Tannhäuser had long forgotten his old life; his friendships, his love for Elizabeth, had alike vanished in the mist which enveloped him, body and soul, when he entered the Venusberg. Sometimes he played on his harp, but none of his old songs came to his memory—all that he sang now were inspired by Venus. Does it not seem sad and terrible that this knight, with his soul full of music and his heart full of love for the beautiful Princess, should have been so cruelly enchanted?

One day Tannhäuser felt suddenly that he was awake once more after a long dream. He told the enchantress, in answer to her questions as to why he was so sad and thoughtful, that he had fancied he heard the distant boom of a far-away church-bell. The sound had pierced the rock walls of the mountain, pierced even the almost impenetrable magic mist, and the faint peal, he said, had reminded him of strange things—the sun, the friendly glimmer of the stars in the far-away heavens, the freshness of the earth at the time of the new summer, the nightingale with his song of spring.

"Are these things lost to me?" asked Tannhäuser.

Rising from the couch upon which she had been reclining, Venus laughed at his words and bade him sing her a song less sad. He obeyed, and accompanying himself on the vibrating strings of his harp, sang a melody which he had learned from the sorceress herself. But the words to which he set the music were but a further expression of longing for the upper earth—for the natural joys and sorrows that belong to a world of men. Again Venus interrupted his song, this time to reproach him for his ingratitude to her for the beautiful things she had lavished upon him since he came to her grotto. Once more Tannhäuser smote his harp. After paying her musical homage, and describing her graciousness to him, and his dreamy life in the Venusberg, he sang new words. The melody, which was very lovely, came from his heart as he sang, and his hands touched the harp-strings softly in accompaniment:

> "In rose-veiled grottos I am longing
> To feel the soft wood-breezes thronging;
> I long for heaven's crystal blue,
> Long for the old earth, fresh anew
> In spring, when wild birds sing of love;
> I long for noon-hot skies above.
> From these, thy splendors, hasten I,
> Oh, Sovereign! Goddess! let me fly!"

His voice rose to passionate pleading with the last words, and his harp fell to the ground; but Venus would not withdraw her spells, nor give consent to his freedom. She spoke to him in soft tones; she promised him more perfect joys, more wondrous flowers, more exquisite music. As she spoke the shadows deepened, the mist glowed more richly, the scent from the heavy-headed flowers grew overpoweringly sweet. From the dim blue lake came the sirens' voices, softly, with wondrous harmonies. They sang of flowers, and noiseless blue waters, and rest, and enchantment. With their voices sounded that of Venus—she was speaking gently.

"My knight," she said, "will you fly?"

Passionately Tannhäuser again seized his harp, and his voice soared out with power and the strings rang beneath his hands. He sang that while he had life and breath he would sing the praises of Venus, and Venus alone. She, and none other, should be his theme—this he vowed, if she would but let him go.

In a voice breaking with anger the enchantress gave him permission to depart, but bade him return if he met with coldness in the upper world. In a moment the grotto and all within it flashed away. . . .

Tannhäuser found himself lying on a grassy

slope, under the wide blue sky, with the sun shining down upon him. On one side was a mountain,
the sight of which made him tremble; on the other
was the Wartburg, stately and grand as ever. From
the high pasture-land above him came the sound of
sheep-bells, and up among the rocks lay a shepherd
boy, playing on his pipe, and pausing now and then
to sing a song of Holda, the goddess of spring. A
band of pilgrims passed on their way to Rome,
chanting a slow, melodious prayer, a grand pæan of
faith which sounded through the valley harmonious-
ly and impressively. They went on their way with
solemn tread, and their voices were lost in the distance. Soon the shepherd collected his flock and,
playing his pipe, vanished from view among the high
bowlders and shrubbery. The knight, left alone,
bowed his head humbly and prayed that he might
by righteous works obtain pardon for the year wasted in the Venusberg. The voices of the pilgrims, a
long way off, were wafted faintly to him once more.
Then the chant and the echoes that it had awakened
mingled and died away. Across the quiet of the
valley came the sound of hunting-horns. They answered each other from all sides — now with single
long-drawn challenging notes, now with short jovial
measures, cheery, and full of a sort of excitement
which seemed new to the lonely knight who listened.
A pack of hunting-dogs bounded down a forest path

before him, followed by the Landgrave and five Minstrel Knights, in hunting-dress.

Passing near Tannhäuser they recognized him at once, and surrounded him, with words of welcome and pleasure. The Landgrave, with much kindness, asked where he had been during the year of his absence.

" I wandered in strange, strange lands," answered Tannhäuser, gloomily, " where I found not the rest that I am now seeking. Question not, but let me depart."

He would have left them without further words, but to the urgent entreaties of all Sir Wolfram von Eschenbach added another more potent persuasion. He told Tannhäuser how sad Elizabeth had been while he was away, how she would not join in the revels nor listen to the minstrelsy. All this moved Tannhäuser's heart deeply, and he started up with eager impatience.

" Guide me to her!" he cried, feeling a thrill of tenderness at the thought of the maiden who had not been in his mind or memory for a long year.

The knight was at last truly happy. The heavens seemed to smile down upon him in pardon ; the sunshine blessed and caressed him, and the soft wind that blew against his face brought him peace and a sense of freedom. As he mounted the steep ascent

towards the castle with his friends, his heart throb-
bed thankfully.

"Guide me to her!" he cried once more, and with
voices full of jubilance and gladness the Landgrave
and his six Minstrel Knights entered the Wartburg.

The Shepherd Boy's Pipe

CHAPTER II

THE CONTEST OF SONG

THE Wartburg was an old and magnificent castle. It had long been the dwelling-place of the Landgraves of Thuringia and the high nobles of the realm. In the castle was a hall, large and lofty, called—because of the musical contests held within it—the Minstrels' Hall. At the back of it nothing, save high pillars, shut out the wide view of the valley.

On the evening of Tannhäuser's home-coming the hall was elaborately decked, in preparation for a contest between the Minstrel Knights. The contest had long been planned, but it was decided to enter Tannhäuser's name among the rest in honor of his return, and also in recognition of his marvellous skill. A little while before the hour appointed for the lyrical battle, the Princess Elizabeth hastened into the hall to gaze on the place where the min-strel's voice and harp had awakened such sympathy in her soul. She had heard of his return, and her heart was beating with tumultuous joy.

The Princess Elizabeth was very beautiful, as a princess should be. She was of northern birth, and had the straight, tall figure, the fair hair, the fresh coloring, and the clear blue eyes with which the daughters of cold skies so often are endowed. She entered swiftly, with firm step, her white soft draperies, embroidered in rich, brilliant colors, falling about her in many folds. Her bright hair was braided in heavy plaits, and a small, low crown of fretted gold marked her Princess of Thuringia. No wonder knights and nobles and princes came from far and wide, suing for her hand in marriage. She was kind to all, but always cold and stately, and though she was gentle and charitable, she was proud also with the pride of many generations of noble blood. Only one knight had ever touched her heart, and during his absence she had resolutely excluded herself from the gayeties of the realm. But now he had returned. All her spirit thrilled with a surge of joy that quickened her heart-beats, and sent a fire of happiness to her blue eyes. So she was standing, a queenly, beautiful figure, when Tannhäuser, led by Wolfram, came from a doorway at the side of the hall into her presence.

"She is there," said Wolfram, softly, and turned away to lean against a carved column, his gaze fixed upon the still beauty of the valley. He heard Tannhäuser cry, "Oh, Princess!" Then, after a moment,

Elizabeth said, softly, "You must not kneel to me."

He heard no more, save now and then a word—"happiness," or "hope"—which made him cover his face with his hands in despair. For Wolfram, too, loved the Princess Elizabeth, and had cherished hopes of winning her. He relinquished all, now, to his friend.

After a while Tannhäuser joined him, embraced him excitedly, and together they left the hall. Elizabeth looked after the two knights for a moment, then as the Landgrave entered the hall she ran to him, and flung herself into his arms.

"Ah," said the Landgrave, smiling, "you will come again to our hall, then, to witness the contest?"

Together they mounted the royal dais, and awaited the arrival of the knights and ladies who had been bidden to the festivities. Four pages announced each guest, and then one after the other they were received by the Landgrave with stately courtesy, and by the Princess with the utmost graciousness, made welcome, and escorted by the pages to their seats in the great rapidly forming semicircle of people. At last all were seated : the knights and ladies in richest mediæval dress, behind them the men-at-arms and attendants, while all the castle retainers stood at the back of the hall. Swinging-

lamps lighted up the stately columns of stone, the
minute and exquisite carvings, the rich coloring of
the guests' apparel, the silver hair of the Landgrave,
and the fair face of the Princess by his side. When
all were seated the Minstrel Knights entered, dressed
as harpers, and carrying their harps in their hands.
First came Tannhäuser. His unusually handsome
face and free carriage, with the memory of his musical skill and his mysterious absence, made him an
object of general interest. Close behind him came
his friend, Wolfram von Eschenbach, a brave knight,
quiet, grave, and poetical by nature, and well beloved. Walther von der Vogelweide followed. He
was one of the greatest of all the Minnesinger of
that day. Biterolf, a brave but rough and hot-head-
ed knight, came next, followed by Heinrich von
Schreiber and Reinmar von Zweiter. Each bowed
low to the Landgrave and the assembly, and was
conducted to his place by the four pages.

Then the Landgrave arose and addressed the
minstrels. He bade them welcome, and spoke of
their achievements in song. He said that the sword
of Germany had remained unbroken before the
southern foes, and that the harp was worthy of equal
honor. All that was good, all that was noble should
be fitted to its strains; it expressed all the sweetest
and best emotions of life. He welcomed Tannhäuser
in especially kindly terms, then proclaimed the theme

of the contest to be "Love," and promised the hand
of Elizabeth to the winner.

There was a general commotion. "All hail to
Thuringia's Sovereign!" cried many voices. Then
came a deep silence, as the four pages advanced
with a golden cup, into which each of the minstrels dropped a folded slip of paper bearing his
name. The pages then carried the cup to Elizabeth,
who drew out one of the slips and gave it to them.
After reading the name upon it they advanced to
the centre of the hall, and spoke in high, clear voices:
" Wolfram von Eschenbach, begin."

There was a hush, during which Wolfram rose
slowly to his feet. Tannhäuser sat silent, as though
in a net of dreams, leaning on his harp.

Making his harpstrings ripple with a restful ca-
dence, Wolfram began to sing. He sang first of the
brave knights and beautiful ladies who were present,
and then addressed Elizabeth, who, he said, shone
upon them like a gentle star. As he looked into her
face, he said, he saw revealed, as in a vision, the
clear Fountain of Love.

As he ended, there were exclamations of approval
and pleasure from the people. Tannhäuser alone
did not join in the applause. As he sat there it
seemed to him that a wreath of rose-colored mist
passed suddenly before his eyes. A swift memory
enchained him. He rose quickly.

4

"I, too, have seen the Fountain of Love," he
cried, "but I cannot understand all that you say,
Wolfram. Only in search for excitement, and in
magical enchantment, have I found love."

He seated himself in silence. No approbation
met his words, for all felt that a spirit of evil, a dark
enchantment, lingered in what he had said. And
indeed it was so. When Tannhäuser was under
the influence of Venus, he did not understand what
love was. He thought it was a sort of spell, magical, unreal, and far removed from love itself. And
that night, strange as it seems, the enchantress's
spells were again about him, and he understood
nothing that was good or noble. And this was the
result of restlessness and a foolish desire for change.
We slip under evil influences, and once there, it is
very hard to escape; and even when we think our-
selves free the old spell comes back, and all that is
best and truest in our hearts is blown away, as
though by winds. But it is possible for us to be
free at last, as you will see in this story.

Walther von der Vogelweide arose, and rebuked
Tannhäuser for his words, assuring him that he
could know nothing of love; that it was neither a
wild excitement nor an enchantment, but something good, and true, and beautiful — something
springing, all purity and tenderness, from the
soul.

" Hail, Walther, good is the song!" cried the nobles.

Tannhäuser rose hastily, but before he could say more than a few words of contempt for Walther's song, Biterolf, starting to his feet, challenged him to a combat, accusing him of insulting Elizabeth by his talk of enchantment and magic, instead of singing to her, the Princess.   In furious excitement the nobles pressed forward.   The two knights had drawn their swords, and were standing with angry faces and eager hands.   The Landgrave spoke to them with stern authority, ordering them to put up their swords, and commanding them to be at peace with each other.   The Princess, who had listened with her face very white, sat silent, her hands clasped convulsively.

Wolfram von Eschenbach again touched his harp, endeavoring by a few quiet words to still the excitement.   He sang with noble fervor to the star of love, ending with these words :

> " Thou, holy Love, inspire me,
> Thy power voice in me ;
> Teach me thy tender music,
> Celestial melody.

> " Thou art by God vouchsafed us,
> Thy light we follow far ;
> On all the lands is shining
> Eternally thy star !"

Tannhäuser sprang to his feet, hardly conscious of what he was doing. He seemed surrounded by wild, unseen influences—voices were in his ears—a dazzling rose-colored light was in his eyes. He stood as though blind, with throbbing heart, swaying like one in a tempest. Then he smote his harp, till the roof rang with the stormy music, and sang. Once, in the Venusberg, he had vowed that when he sang Venus and none other should be his theme. Now he kept his word. Higher, clearer, louder rose his voice, in a wild eulogy of Venus, Goddess of Love, and mightiest of all enchantresses. At last he flung his harp away, crying, "Fly! Fly to the Venusberg!" and stood transfixed, as though in a trance, his harp unnoticed at his feet.

With anger and indignation the nobles pressed forward, crying in horror-stricken tones, "Listen! Hear him! He has been in the Venusberg!"

Elizabeth stood shuddering, and clinging to a pillar, but all the other ladies hastened from the hall in terror and dismay, leaving the knights to gather about the minstrel and upbraid him in words of horror and hatred. "Send him away — miserable creature!" they cried. "Disown him—in his blood bathe every sword!"

The clamor rose to a tumult, as one and all caught up the cry, and "Kill him!" sounded on every side. The knights, drawing their swords, closed about

"I PLEAD FOR HIM—I PLEAD FOR HIS LIFE."

Tannhäuser to slay him. Suddenly a figure in trailing draperies rushed the length of the hall, and threw herself in front of the offender.

"Stop!" cried Elizabeth, in tones of mingled despair and command. "Stand back!—or else kill me."

The knights whispered together, amazed. Never could they have believed that the Princess would have stooped to shield one like Tannhäuser. Elizabeth continued, her voice full of piteous tragedy, "What is the wound that your swords could give to the death-stroke that has been dealt me?"

"You indeed should be the first to scorn and reproach him," cried the nobles.

"Why do you speak of me?" said the Princess, with passionate sadness. "You should speak of him —his salvation. Would you rob him of his eternal hope of forgiveness from God?"

"He cannot be forgiven!" shouted the knights, rushing forward with their swords ready to strike, but Elizabeth's voice again restrained them.

"Away!" she cried, indignantly, "how dare you judge him? Against your swords he has but one."

She checked her own excitement and continued more gently, all her soul pleading in her voice:

"Hear through me what must be God's will. This unfortunate one, who has found himself held by the terrible magic—can he not win forgiveness

in this world through repentance and sorrow? If
you are so strong in holy faith, do you not know
the highest command—to be merciful, and comfort
grief? I plead for him—I plead for his life."

Tannhäuser bowed his head in his hands, overpowered by her words and his own remorse. The
knights, softened and touched, drew near him, talking together, and speaking to him more gently but
always with reproach. At last the Landgrave, with
slow tread, stepped into the centre of the crowd, and
in grave, sad words, told Tannhäuser that he must be
banished from the realm. Around him clung magic
spells, and dark enchantment lingered in his heart.
He and the evil influences about him must depart
from Thuringia, and he must not return until he
should be himself once more, and free from all the
magical chains of Venus. He earnestly advised
Tannhäuser to join the band of pilgrims who were
about to start for Rome, to obtain pardon for all
their sins from the Pope. All the knights united in
entreating Tannhäuser to do this, and strengthen-
ing their appeals came a slow, sweet chant from
without. The pilgrims were preparing to set forth
on their journey. Their voices fell with restful
power upon the confusion in the Minstrels' Hall.
Tannhäuser's face brightened as he listened, and,
with a wild, hopeful impulse, he cried, "To Rome!"
and rushed out of the hall to join the pilgrims.

The Landgrave and Elizabeth, with the minstrels and nobles, followed him to the great doorway of the hall, speeding him with eager gestures of encouragement and hope, and echoing as with one voice, "To Róme!"

CHAPTER III

THE POPE'S STAFF

FULL of hope, repentance, and longing for pardon,
Tannhäuser hastened on his pilgrimage to Rome.
The road was long and rough, and, like the other
pilgrims, he walked all the way with no aid save his
staff; but his own remorse, his new-born faith in
God, and the reverent love which he felt for Elizabeth made the road easy, and helped him to find
comfort in all his privations. When he saw the other
pilgrims choose the smooth way over the meadow-
land, he turned aside to bruise his feet among sharp
rocks and brambles; when they paused to drink at
streams by the wayside, he endured his thirst in silence and pressed on. His sorrow and contrition
were complete. He was strangely altered from the
knight who sang in the Wartburg. He felt changed;
older, and graver, and full of noble thoughts for

future deeds. Many of the pilgrims rested at the
Hospice, but he remained outside in the snow, happy
in bearing the cold and watching the stars glimmer
in the dark sky.

At last, after many days, he reached Rome. The
bells were pealing, voices were singing anthems, and
the day rose on the weary band of pilgrims as
though with a promise of pardon. One by one they
went into the presence of the Pope; one by one
they returned, with his assurance that God would
forgive them for all their sins. Then came Tannhäuser's turn. He knelt humbly, and told of all his
foolishness, his wasted year, and the evil spells which
had surrounded him, and which had seized him so
wildly that night in the Minstrels' Hall. Sternly
the Pope answered him:

"If you have been in the Venusberg you will
never be free from the magic powers. If you have
been enchained once by the spell you will succumb
to it again. Freedom from enchantment and forgiveness from God you may hope for on that day on
which my bare staff shall put forth green leaves."

Dumb with despair, Tannhäuser staggered away,
and sank down upon the hard earth overpowered by
the hopelessness of what had been told him. After
a time he rose, to find that he was alone. The pilgrims had passed on their way towards home. From
afar sounded their chorus of thanksgiving for their

pardon. Tannhäuser took up his staff and started on his journey alone, without consolation or hope.

*   *   *   *   *   *

A year had passed since Tannhäuser had set out upon his pilgrimage. Every day Elizabeth prayed for him at a shrine to the Virgin, in the valley. Every day Wolfram, watching, saw the longing in her eyes, the growing sadness that preyed upon her, the anxiety that made her face white and sorrowful.

It was sunset in the valley below the Wartburg. As Elizabeth came to kneel at the shrine she seemed more troubled and disturbed than usual, and Wolfram knew that she realized how near it was to the time when the pilgrims must be expected to return. He was passing slowly down a forest path, looking now and then towards the white kneeling figure, when from the distance the pilgrims' chorus made him stop abruptly. Elizabeth started to her feet, with clasped hands, whispering, " It is their song!"

Nearer and nearer came the pilgrims, singing of God's mercy and forgiveness, and the blessedness of pardon. They came in sight; Elizabeth strained her eyes to see the face of the pilgrim whom she loved and for whom she prayed; they passed, and were gone from sight, singing triumphantly.

" He will never return," said Elizabeth, quietly, and as the chant died away she sank on her knees in

"ELIZABETH CAME TO KNEEL AT THE SHRINE"

prayer. After a few minutes she rose, and passed on her way towards the Wartburg.

"May I not go with you?" asked Wolfram, gently, coming forward in sorrow and pity. She shook her head, looking at him with eyes full of gratitude, and an exaltation which startled him. Raising her hand, she pointed upward, stood motionless a moment, then slowly mounted the steep pathway leading to the castle, and was gone. Wolfram stood looking after her until she was out of sight, then he seated himself among some high rocks and struck his harp. Numberless thoughts passed through his mind, born of the coming night with its all-shadowing wings of gloom. He sang softly a song in which he made Elizabeth and the pure evening star one beautiful shining spirit. Then he ceased singing and sat silent, playing on his harp among the shadows.

The night came down, dark and lowering. From the upper end of the valley came a figure with uncertain steps. It was that of a pilgrim, in ragged garb, leaning heavily on his staff. As he drew near, Wolfram recognized the wasted face and burning eyes to be those of Tannhäuser, and started forward.

"What does this mean?" he cried. "Why do you look so despairing? Did you not receive pardon? Speak! tell me all! Have you not been in Rome?"

"Yes," said Tannhäuser, bitterly, " I have been in Rome."

" Unfortunate one," said Wolfram, sadly, "I am waiting in deepest pity to hear the narrative of your pilgrimage."

Tannhäuser looked up, astonished at the gentleness of the words. Then seating himself upon a rock he told the story of his journey to Rome and repeated the words of the Pope. As he completed the narrative he rose to his feet with determination. A memory had come to him of Venus's bidding to return to her if the world met him with coldness. The Pope had assured him that there was no hope for him; then why not voluntarily throw himself beneath the sorceress's spell, since he could never escape from it, even by earnest endeavor? In the Venusberg the turmoil and struggle in his heart would be stilled, and he longed to hear the rich music and see the rosy mists sinking down over the still waters, and breathe the sweet, heavy perfume of the flowers.

"I have tried to do my best," he cried, suddenly. " I have toiled, with suffering and penitence, to over-come the evil spells that were about me. Men have turned from me and refused me their help. They have told me that I could never be free from the enchantment. So what does it matter? Come, Venus — enchantress, sorceress, marvellous goddess ! —

"HE REACHED THE BIER WITH DIFFICULTY"

come and show me the path by which I may return
to the Venusberg!"

As he spoke great clouds rolled from above and
below and from all sides, surrounding him and Wolfram. Winds heavy with fragrance blew through
the darkness ; piercingly sweet music came to them ;
brilliant, rosy light gleamed in the midst of the
clouds, which glowed in answering brightness until it
was as though a surging, rolling sea of rose-color filled
the air. Misty figures appeared in the magical glow,
dancing in dizzy circles through the clouds. The
doors of the Venusberg seemed to have been
opened. Within Venus was seen beckoning in the
radiance. Her voice came softly, caressingly to
the ears of Tannhäuser, but he was closely held
by Wolfram and could not go. At last, after a
fierce struggle, he tore himself free and started forward.

"Wait—wait," panted Wolfram, with exalted appeal, "God will pardon you! An angel even now
is pleading for you in heaven—Elizabeth."

Tannhäuser started, as though a knife had been
thrust suddenly into his heart.

"Elizabeth!" he repeated, in hushed tones, and
there came into his heart a strange, new sensation of
freshness and peace, together with a great, overwhelming sorrow. The light upon the mist faded,
the magic music ceased. From the castle came a

train of people, bearing torches and singing an an-
them in solemn voices.

"Alas," cried the sorceress, wildly, "I have lost
him !"

She sank into the earth, the doors of the Venusberg crashed together, the mist vanished, and from
over the hills shone the first light of the dawn.

"Do you hear the music?" whispered Wolfram.

"I hear it," answered Tannhäuser, with bowed
head.

Higher rose the voices in the fresh morning air as
a number of knights came down the path from the
Wartburg bearing a bier. Upon it lay Elizabeth,
who in prayer and sorrow for Tannhäuser had died.
In response to a gesture from Wolfram the bier was
placed upon the ground and Tannhäuser was led
slowly to it by his friend, for all his strength seemed
suddenly to have left him. He reached it with difficulty, and sank quietly to the earth, putting out
his hands as though in reverent supplication.

"Holy Elizabeth, pray for me !" he whispered. He
sank back. The knights, drawing near, saw that he
was dead. One by one the torches were extinguished. Suddenly came the sound of voices singing of the marvel wrought by God: the Pope's
staff had put forth new green leaves, and he had
sent it by messengers out over the land, to bring to
the banished pilgrim the proof of his pardon. One

and all raised their voices in a stupendous pæan of prayerful thanksgiving for Tannhäuser's freedom from evil spells, and for God's mercy to him.

Over the valley the sunshine streamed out brilliantly, gloriously, as though in fulfilment of the promise of the dawn.

The Pilgrims' Chorus

LOHENGRIN

Elsa's Dream Motif

CHAPTER I

THE COMING OF THE KNIGHT

WE read in an old legend of a cup in which Jesus
Christ's blood was received when He hung, wounded
to death, upon the Cross. Angels took the cup,
which had been made sacred forever, and placed it
in a secret shrine, in a castle named Monsalvat,
where it was worshipped by a mystic Brotherhood
of Knights. The cup was called the Holy Grail,
and those who guarded it became immortal through
its power. Once every year it was unveiled, and a
white dove flew down from heaven and hovered
over it; at other times it was kept concealed in its
shrine, worshipped by all the Knights of Monsalvat.
It is this legend that forms the background for the
story which I shall tell you.

In the first half of the tenth century Germany
was at war with the Hungarians, who threatened in-
vasion. The King of Germany, Heinrich I., often

called Der Vogler (the Fowler), hastened to Brabant
to collect forces to assist in repelling the invaders,
and also to sit in judgment upon disputes, as was
his annual custom. Arriving at Antwerp, he found
that the duchy was in a much confused state, with
apparently no one governing it.

Upon a bright clear day he made his way to the
banks of the Scheldt, where a throne had been placed
for him in the shade of a great tree called the Oak
of Justice. Looking around him upon the assembled
Brabantians, and the many Saxons and Thuringians
who were also present, he caught sight of the dark
features of one who had saved his life in a battle
with the Danes—a noble of Brabant, well-reputed in
war and peace, Friedrich, Count von Telramund.
On being called upon to give an explanation of the
strange condition of affairs in the duchy, Count von
Telramund stepped forward.

He was a tall man with frowning brows and som-
bre black eyes, and wore the rich robes indicating
the state of a Brabantian duke. Behind him stood
his wife, silent and watchful.

"I am thankful, my King," said Telramund, with
ill-concealed excitement, "that you have come to
judge us of Brabant. I will tell you the truth.
When our Duke lay dying he chose me as guardian
of his children— Elsa, a maiden, and Gottfried, a
boy. I guarded them with care during their child-

hood; their life was dearer to me than my honor. Hear, my King, how I have been wronged! Elsa and the boy went gayly wandering into the wood one day. She returned without him, saying that they had become separated, and beseeching us to tell her what we knew of him, and her lamentations and feigned anxiety were great. Fruitless was all our search and all our mourning. I spoke sternly to Elsa, and by her blanched lips and shudderings she was betrayed. Her appearance of horror and fear confessed to me the girl's guilt. Her father had willed me her hand in marriage, but I thankfully relinquished the right, and chose a wife who pleased me well—Ortrud, Princess of Friesland, and daughter of the brave Radbod."

He turned towards his wife, and she came forward, bowing low before the King. She was very handsome, with a gleam in her eyes like that of a watching lioness. Upon her head was the coronet of Brabant, and her carriage was that of a queen. A beautiful, brave, but treacherous woman was Ortrud, Countess von Telramund.

"I herewith charge Elsa of Brabant with fratricide!" continued Friedrich, loudly. "And because my wife comes of the race from which this land received its rulers long ago, and because I am the nearest kinsman of our brave dead Duke, I claim dominion over the duchy of Brabant."

As Count von Telramund ended his story, quick
exclamations of amazement and horror were heard
on all sides. The King himself was troubled and
incredulous, and declared that he would not cease
endeavors until the truth had been determined and
justice dealt. The herald came forward and called,
in loud tones, upon the Princess Elsa of Brabant to
come before the King for judgment.

There was a hush—every one waited breathlessly.
Soon, at the edge of the crowd, soft words could be
heard passing from lip to lip.

"Behold her—she comes nearer! How fair and
pure and sweet she seems! Oh, the truth must be
disclosed!"

The people parted eagerly before the train of ladies who slowly made their way towards the throne.
All were fair, and robed in pale blue and pure
white, to symbolize the innocence of their mistress.
Among them, dressed simply in white, with her
bright golden hair streaming about her pale face
and a dreamy light in her deep-blue eyes, walked
Elsa, the young Duchess of Brabant, uncrowned and
humbled before her subjects, yet seeming a princess
still, refuting all accusations by the sweetness and
simple majesty of her demeanor. Her ladies remained with the crowd, and she came forward alone
to receive judgment.

"Are you Elsa of Brabant?" asked the King.

"Are you prepared to be judged by me? Can you meet the accusation that is made against you?"

Elsa met each of these questions with silence. Her dreamy eyes were turned with a rapt gaze to the far blue of the distant hills.

" Then," resumed the King—" then you confess your guilt?"

Elsa raised her eyes to his.

" My poor brother!" she whispered, with lingering sadness, and was again silent. There was a general murmur of astonishment—the people were bewildered.

"Speak, Elsa," said the King, gently. " What do you wish to confide in me?"

Every one listened eagerly, as slowly and very softly Elsa began to speak.

" When I have been lonely, I have often prayed for help," she said, in low, hushed tones. " It came when I could not know it was so near. It was while I was asleep."

She did not raise her voice, but a note of exaltation crept into it, and the words which followed were full of triumphant solemnity.

" I saw in shining clouds of glory the figure of a knight. The brightness of his countenance was marvellous, and he leaned upon a glittering sword. In a low, tender voice he spoke words of comfort,

and I awoke, filled with hope.   He will defend me—
he will be my champion !"

Her voice rang more clearly with the last words,
and struck a conviction of truth to all who heard.

" Friedrich," said the King, solemnly, " think,
while there is yet time.   In the name of all honor,
do you still accuse her ?"

" I have proof," answered Friedrich von Telramund, firmly.   " I have as witness one who knows.
But let any one who still believes not stand forth
and fight with me, and may Heaven aid the
right !"

The people assented, with murmurs of approval,
and the King spoke with great gravity.

" I ask you, Friedrich, Count von Telramund, will
you do battle here, for life or death, and allow
Heaven to decide the truth by the conqueror ?"

" Yes," said Telramund, defiantly.

" And now I ask you, Elsa of Brabant, will you
submit to Heaven's decision in the battle for life or
death ?"

" Yes," whispered Elsa, softly ; and in answer to
the King's question as to her champion, she said
that she would place her trust in the mysterious
Knight of her dream ; he, she declared, would defend her.

This, you know, was the ancient way of determin-
ing questions of right and wrong.   Champions

fought, each for his cause, calling upon Heaven to favor the truth.

It was now mid-day. At the King's command, four trumpeters placed themselves at the four points of the compass, and blew long and loud. The herald took his stand in front of the King's throne, and cried:

"Let him stand forth who will do battle before God for Elsa of Brabant."

There was a long, strained silence. No response came to the summons.

"There is no answer," muttered the people, uneasily.

"You see how she stands convicted before God!" cried Friedrich von Telramund, exultantly.

"Oh, my beloved King," besought Elsa, turning pleadingly to the throne, "summon my Knight again! He dwells afar and does not hear."

"Once more sound the call," commanded the King, and the summons was repeated. As a second silence followed the first, there was a general movement of disappointment and uneasiness. Telramund raised his head triumphantly.

Dropping on her knees, Elsa prayed with her whole soul for the help which had been promised her. One by one, all her ladies did likewise, praying earnestly for justice and aid.

Every heart beat with intense excitement, born

of the suspense. The situation was painful in its expectancy, yet seeming hopelessness ; not the faintest rustle could be heard in the crowd, so deep was the stillness.

Suddenly, from the men nearest the water's edge, came a wild cry :

" See ! see ! What is this? A swan ! A swan comes near, drawing a boat ! Within the craft stands a knight. How his armor gleams! The swan is harnessed with a golden chain. See, nearer comes the marvel !"

" A wonder — a wonder !" shouted the people, rushing to the edge of the shore. " A wonder is come !"

The King from his high throne watched the approach of the Knight with amazement and joy. Telramund started at the cries of the men, but Ortrud remained silent, haughty, and seemingly unheeding, until she saw the stately swan which drew the boat. As her eyes caught sight of the soft plumage and crested neck of the beautiful bird she grew rigid with horror, and when she perceived the curious golden chain with which it was bridled, she shrank as from a threatening sword.

Elsa, with a soft, joyful cry, rose from her knees, gazing in worship upon the Knight, who now sprang on shore. His armor, fashioned of pure silver, reflected the light brilliantly ; the upper part of his

helmet was carved in the form of a swan with outstretched, shining wings; from his shoulder hung a
cloak of clear blue, the color of the sky; a shield
covered with strange designs hung behind him; a
golden horn hung at his belt; his gauntleted hand
grasped the hilt of a sword. He was tall and powerful, with deep golden hair and beard, the brightness of which seemed like a nimbus of sunshine
about his face. His forehead was broad, his eyes
deep and far-seeing, and about him lingered a mystic glory, new to the eyes of the people who watched
him. They grew hushed and awed after the first
clamor of relief. Helmets were doffed in homage,
and the hearts of one and all went out in instinctive
respect, admiration, and love to the stranger Knight.

Turning to his swan, he spoke to it in words of
tenderness, and after thanking it for drawing the
craft so safely and well, bade it farewell in tones full
of regret at the parting.

"Farewell, farewell, my beloved swan!" he ended,
softly. With lowered head, and every sign of sorrow, the mystical bird floated away, drawing the
craft along the water's shining path, until the snow-
white form vanished in the winding curves of the
river.

The Knight turned from the water's side, and advancing with a buoyant step to the throne, cried in
a clear voice:

"Hail, King Heinrich! May your valor, justice, and honor have meet reward!"

"You have my thanks," returned the King, courteously. "I must believe," he added, questioningly, "that you are sent by Heaven to fulfil a mission?"

"Yes," responded the Knight, "I have come to do battle before God for this maiden with whoever accuses her."

He turned swiftly to where Elsa was standing. "So speak, Elsa of Brabant!" he cried. "Will you trust your cause to my strength in battle without fear?"

"My hero! My rescuer!" whispered Elsa, brokenly. "Protect me, and I—I give you all that I have or am."

"If I conquer in battle for you," continued the Knight, "will you pledge me your faith?"

"Bending at your feet, I will give you all my heart and soul," answered the girl, steadily.

"Elsa," said the Knight, tenderly, "if you plight me your troth, if I conquer for you, if we are united forever—then a promise I must exact from you." He paused a moment, then spoke gravely, impressively: "Never must you question me, nor covet the knowledge of my name nor my home nor my race."

"Never, my lord, will I question you," replied Elsa.

"'I HAVE COME TO DO BATTLE BEFORE GOD FOR THIS MAIDEN'"

Anxiously the Knight repeated his command, begging her to think well before promising.

"My shield! My protector!" said Elsa, simply. "As you have trusted and defended me, so will I hold myself true and obedient to your behest."

Advancing towards her the Knight took her hands in his.

"Elsa, I love you," he said; and the people, unable to keep silence longer, burst into words of delight and of complete trust in the stranger Knight.

"Now hear!" he cried, turning towards them, his clear voice making itself heard by every one. "To you, nobles and people of Brabant, I make this known: Free from all guilt is Elsa of Brabant, and, Count von Telramund, your accusation is false. Before God you shall retract it!"

The Brabantian nobles surrounded Telramund, endeavoring to dissuade him from the combat, for which he had begun to prepare.

"Heaven has sent him," they urged. "Oh, surrender without blood!"

"I love death better than submission," returned Friedrich, frowning angrily. "Stranger, whatever magic sent you here, I shall conquer, if victory attends the right."

At the King's command, three knights came forward for each warrior, and measured the ground for the combat. They then took their stand in the front

of the crowd, a regular number of feet apart, the
six thus forming a complete circle, and drove their
spears into the ground. The King then proclaimed
the circle to be a field of battle, and the herald came
forward. He pronounced the ground to be for the
combatants only, and threatened dire punishment
on him who dared break the circle, or in any way
hinder the battle ; he enjoined the warriors to con-
duct themselves nobly in fair battle, to use no magic,
and to submit to and abide by the divine decision.
All bent their heads in prayer for some minutes;
then, in the midst of a breathless excitement, the
trumpeters blew the battle-call.

The two knights completed their preparations and
stood ready to enter the circle. The King struck
his shield three times with his sword. With the
first stroke they swiftly took their places ; with the
second stroke each moved forward a step, his shield
on his arm and his sword drawn and presented ;
with the third and last stroke the combat began.

The stranger Knight attacked, and after a few
passes struck his adversary to the earth ; then, al-
though he held the right to slay his fallen enemy,
he drew back, leaving him prostrate. Telramund
rose, staggered, and though not seriously hurt, fell
back again, overcome with humiliation. In the
noise of acclamation which followed, he dragged
himself to Ortrud's feet, and remained there, bowed

and stricken with despair. She wrung her hands passionately, without sympathy for him, but full of angry disappointment.

"Oh, shame!" she muttered. "Is this the end of all my hopes?"

Meanwhile, oblivious to the misery of Telramund and Ortrud, the Brabantians, frantic with delight and excitement, had raised the Knight upon his shield, and their young Duchess upon the shield of the King, and now bore them away, with a glad chorus of rejoicing.

Swan Music

Motif of Warning

CHAPTER II

BEFORE THE MINSTER

THE royal fortress at Antwerp was divided into the Pallas, the abode of the knights ; the Kemmenate, the residence of the ladies ; the dwellings of the men-at-arms and servants ; and the Minster, a majestic building, in which were held all religious and state ceremonies. On the evening following the coming of the Knight, Friedrich von Telramund and his wife Ortrud were seated upon the steps of the Minster. They were dressed in the rough garments worn only by beggars and wanderers. Friedrich, crushed still by the weight of his degradation, sat in deep and unhappy meditation. Ortrud gazed constantly at the windows of the Pallas, through which poured brilliant light and gay music, telling of the festivities within.

"Arouse yourself," said Telramund, low and gloomily. "When the day dawns we must not be here."

"Nay," returned his wife, "I wait — to be revenged."

" You strange, cruel woman !" cried Friedrich, in
sudden excitement. " Was it not through you that
we met this disgrace ? It was you who gave me
proofs of the maiden's guilt. Did you lie, or did
you speak truth ?"

And now the time has come when we should understand some of these dark mysteries. The Lady
Ortrud, before her marriage, had dwelt in a towered
castle in the heart of the gloomy wood where Elsa
and little Gottfried had wandered on that fateful
day. It was whispered that the castle was the scene
of strange magic rites and spells, and that the lady
who dwelt there was both witch and prophetess.
She had come to Count Telramund with a terrible
tale of a sight seen from her tower window—the
stealthy figure of Elsa of Brabant, who came behind
her brother as he stood on the brink of the castle
moat, and pushed him in. She further told strange
secrets of the future, which had been revealed to
her through her magic powers. The race of Radbod, now almost extinct, would rise again, she said,
and rule two lands—Friesland and Brabant. She
had easily won the belief of the Count, and, moreover, his ambition was excited. As for her story
about Elsa, he accepted it as absolute truth, and
even after his defeat believed that justice had been
conquered by sorcery. Ortrud was clever as well
. as beautiful, and tenacious to her purpose. That

6

purpose was to attain the government of Brabant, and to introduce the old worship of gods in place of Christianity. Ortrud remained true to the great deities adored by her race, and she believed that they bestowed her mystic powers of evil as a means of destroying all enemies and those who stood between her and her desires.

To Telramund's question as to whether she had spoken truth or falsehood, when instigating him to the persecution of Elsa, she replied in short, bitter words of scorn, taunting him with his easy overthrowal in the combat, laughing at his remaining evidences of honorable regret, and finally declaring that she could show him means to overcome the stranger Knight.

"Look!" she said, at last, leaning forward and smiling secretly in the darkness. "They are extinguishing the lights there in the Pallas. The feast is over, the music has ceased, and they are at rest. Come, sit beside me."

Mechanically obeying her beckoning hand, Telramund, who had been pacing to and fro while she spoke, returned, and seated himself upon the steps below her.

"The time is come," said Ortrud, mysteriously, "when I read the stars, and gather my hoards of mystic wisdom. Tell me, does any one know who this Knight is?"

" No," returned Telramund, in a whisper.

" He is helped by magic ; but the spell can be broken if he is obliged to answer the three questions which he has forbidden. Elsa must be the one to ask them."

" How can she be persuaded to break her word ?" asked Telramund, with eagerness.

" We must kindle her suspicions," declared Ortrud, swiftly, " and we must go forth and proclaim to every one the fact that he has won by sorcery."

" Yes, it must have been sorcery," muttered Friedrich.

" I understand many things," whispered Ortrud, with significance, " and I know that any one who works by magic can be rendered helpless if one drop of his blood be spilled."

" Ah," cried Telramund, sharply, " if that be true !" Then he turned fiercely upon her. " If you are deceiving me again, woe for you !"

" You are raving," said Ortrud, contemptuously. " I will but teach you the pleasure of the gods—revenge."

At that moment a door opened and a woman came out on to a balcony on the Kemmenate, and, advancing to the parapet, rested her arm upon it and her head upon her hand. It was Elsa, passing in happy vigil her bridal eve, for the next day she was to wed her knight in the Minster. The moonlight shone upon the bright hair hanging loose over her robe, the soft winds blew against her face, and to the night she confided her gladness.

" It is she," whispered Ortrud, harshly. " Go! Leave her to me!" Telramund crept out of sight among the shadows. Ortrud advanced with a stealthy step until she was under the balcony.

" Elsa!" she cried, her voice sounding weird in the darkness.

Much bewildered, Elsa leaned over the parapet, and, straining her eyes in the dim light, recognized the wife of the man who had so greatly wronged her. "Is it indeed you, unfortunate woman?" she said, pityingly.

Lowly bending, as though in deep contrition and sadness, Ortrud assured her of the regret which tore her husband's heart for the wrong which he had done her, and besought her forgiveness for him. She added that though she herself had never harmed Elsa, she had been banished from her high position with her husband, and shared with him all his hardships and his remorse.

" I am so happy, how can I let unhappiness go uncomforted?" said Elsa, softly. "Wait, Ortrud." She hastily entered the Kemmenate. Ortrud sprang from her kneeling posture.

" Now, my gods," she cried, " grant me your aid, and help me to accomplish my revenge!"

"THE DUCHESS OF BRABANT WITH OUTSTRETCHED HANDS BIDDING
ORTRUD ENTER"

The great door of the Kemmenate swung open, two servants appeared bearing torches, and behind them came the Duchess of Brabant with outstretched hands bidding Ortrud enter, with gentle words of welcome. Checking the assurances of humble gratitude which met her, Elsa promised that she would sue for pardon for Ortrud and her husband on the morrow, and she concluded by bidding the Countess array herself in rich attire, to follow her to the alter on the coming day.

"Only in one way can I requite you," said Ortrud, with hypocritical gratitude, " and that is by making use of my poor powers of prophecy in your behalf. Oh, do not trust too blindly, nor love too well ! I hope — that he who was sent you by magic—" she paused for a moment—"may never leave you."

Smiling, Elsa assured her that her trust was too deep for doubt to disturb it. Then, with the utmost tenderness, she led Ortrud in, and the door was closed.

" There entered the powers of evil !" muttered Friedrich von Telramund, lurking in the shadows. " May they prosper, and overthrow my enemies !"

The dawn broke. Two warders appeared on the ramparts of the Pallas and blew the reveille on their trumpets. Telramund concealed himself behind one of the carved pillars of the Minster. The warders descended a flight of steps and unlocked the gates.

The fortress was now astir, and busy life filled the morning. Various knights soon appeared, and finally the herald came out from the Pallas with his trumpeters. He proclaimed that Friedrich von Telramund was banished and exiled, and that the stranger Knight would hereafter take the title of Protector of Brabant, having refused to accept the name or state of Duke. On that day he would wed the Duchess of Brabant, and on the morrow would stand ready to lead the Brabantians to battle against the invaders.

As the herald finished the proclamation, four pages descended the steps leading from the balcony of the Kemmenate to the ground, crying, " Make way for our Lady Elsa, who goes to the Minster to pray !" Behind the pages came Elsa's ladies, all in the richest of court dresses; they walked two-by-two, and, on reaching the ground, they formed an aisle through which the Duchess was to pass.

Looking very fair and stately in her bridal dress, Elsa came slowly down the steps, followed by a few chosen ladies of high degree, among the foremost of whom was the Countess Ortrud von Telramund. Elsa descended amid a clamor of welcome and adoration, and, looking about her with a soft color in her face, passed on to the Minster. Close behind her walked the Countess von Telramund, and as the Duchess placed her foot upon the lowest step of the

Minster, Ortrud swept before her, claimed prece-
dence, and commanded Elsa to follow her. Being
met with a chorus of amazed derision, she entirely
lost her self-control, and broke into words of stormy
anger, declaring that her husband had been unjust-
ly conquered, and taunting Elsa with the mystery
which hung over the stranger Knight.

Elsa, full of indignation, answered her hotly and
reproachfully, saying that the Knight had been
given fair victory by God, and accusing Ortrud of
slander.

At the same instant the people shouted, " Make
way, make way, the King comes !"

The royal procession which now issued from the
Pallas was stopped by the commotion before it, and
seeing that there was a general disturbance, the
King and the stranger Knight came forward. While
the King questioned the people the Knight made
his way to Elsa's side, and received from her an explanation of the event which had delayed her procession as well as that of the King.

Commanding Ortrud to stand aside, the Knight
took Elsa's hand, and, escorted by the King, they
went towards the Minster, and a second attempt was
made to enter. From within, the chords of the organ could be heard, pealing forth in salutation.
Slowly the procession formed and advanced in time
to the music. Once more the bride's foot was upon

the step, once more she started back in horror, for at the door stood Friedrich von Telramund, crying, "Oh, King, deceived lady, wait!"

Now thoroughly incensed, King Heinrich bade him to begone in a voice of thunder, assuring the Knight that the attempts of this enemy to poison their hearts against him would be useless, and declaring that Friedrich was unbelieved by all. Many of the nobles hastened forward, to press the stranger Knight's hands in expression of their trust.

While he, deeply touched, spoke words of gratitude to them, Telramund crept to Elsa's side and told her that he had a secret which he wished to confide to her. Shuddering, Elsa commanded him to leave her, but he pressed nearer, and, speaking in a hurried whisper, told her that if but one drop of the Knight's blood were spilled he would confess all his past, and, moreover, would be obliged to stay with her forever. Then, while Elsa faintly whispered, "Forever!" he swiftly left her, and the Knight came to her side.

Led by the King, the bridal pair mounted the steps of the Minster. The doors opened wide to receive them, the organ-tones rolled out upon the air in the rich harmonies of the wedding-march.

At the door-way the Knight paused and clasped Elsa in his arms. She raised her eyes and saw beyond him the face of Ortrud, who stood at the foot of the steps, with uplifted hand and a smile of ominous triumph upon her lips. Trembling, Elsa turned away and entered the Minster.

Wedding-March

CHAPTER III

THE THREE QUESTIONS

The long wedding-day was over. The feasting was ended, the merriment stilled. The King, according to the mediæval custom, accompanied, with his retinue, the Knight and his young wife to the bridal chamber. Then he clasped their hands together, and blessed them, and the ladies sang a soft joyful wedding-song, as at last every one went away, leaving the Knight and Elsa alone.

The room was lofty and full of shadows. Torches set in stationary sockets sent a dim flickering light over the stone floor and walls and the rich hangings. At one side was an oriel window, through which streamed the pale moonlight.

When the last sound of the singing had died away, the Knight spoke to Elsa tenderly, telling her that not only had God sent him to be her champion,

but the power of love as well had led him to her.
Elsa answered that she had loved him since she saw
him in her dream ; but she ended, a faint note of sadness coming into her voice, with words of longing,
a deep desire to know those mysteries which he concealed from her.

"Elsa!" said the Knight, sorrowfully. But she continued, with piteous eagerness, "My name sounds so
sweet from your lips," she whispered. "Can you
deny me the melody of yours?"

In answer, the Knight led her silently to the open
window. Before them lay the land, masked in dim-
ness ; dark and mysterious lay the shadows everywhere ; the scent of many flowers came to them,
borne by the night wind.

"Breathe this fragrance," said the Knight, gently.
"It brings a strange happiness ; and if one knew
whence it came, could it be sweeter? I am bound
to you by just such enchantment ; when I did not
know who you were I still loved you, and unques-
tioningly believed in your truth. These scent-laden
winds bring me joy as they reach me in the darkness, and so was I touched by your innocence and
beauty when you were in the black shadow of suspicion."

"Ah," sighed Elsa, "if you could but trust me
enough to confide in me! You would find my power of secrecy great."

"I have asked your love and belief in me," said the Knight, gravely. "Do not doubt me, my wife. I leave nothing of shame behind me. I come to you from happiness, not darkness or sorrow."

"Ah," cried Elsa, with a gesture of passionate despair, "you still long for the joy you have left behind you! I see that you will soon grow weary, and wish to return to it. Oh, how can I bind you to me? You are surrounded by magic, you came to me through a spell! How can I be rid of all doubt? How can I have surety?"

As she spoke she fancied that she heard a step without. "Did you hear nothing?" she whispered. "Did you hear no one coming?"

Then suddenly she grew rigid, motionless, staring before her as though she saw a vision.

"Ah!" she gasped, under her breath. "There—the swan—the swan! It comes nearer—there, swimming over the flowing waters! It comes for you! It is drawing the boat hither!"

"Elsa," said the Knight, anxiously, "calm yourself; banish your dreams." But, almost beside herself, she turned wildly towards him:

"Hear me, for I must question you!" she cried. "Tell me your name!"

"Forbear!"

"Where is your home?"

"Alas—alas!" he exclaimed, sorrowfully.

"What is your race?" cried Elsa, in desperation.

At the same moment Friedrich von Telramund, with four nobles who had joined him in his evil errand, entered noiselessly through a door at the farther end of the room. Perceiving them, Elsa at once recollected herself, and catching up her husband's sword, which had been removed, held it out to him, crying, "Save yourself!"

With the weapon in his hand he turned and struck at his enemy in time to save himself from the uplifted blade, which now fell with a ring on the floor, as Telramund sank dead at the feet of the Knight. The four nobles flung away their swords, and knelt before him to whom Heaven had again given victory.

"Bear him to the King," he said, quietly; and lifting their burden, the nobles departed.

Elsa had sunk fainting upon the Knight's arm. He raised her gently, and carried her to the couch, where he laid her, sighing, "Alas, all our happiness is gone!"

Elsa turned her face to the pillow in despair, praying brokenly in a whisper. The Knight struck a bell, and as one of Elsa's ladies appeared, he bade her make the Duchess ready to go before the King.

"There," he said, slowly and sadly, "I will reveal all she asks."

As the lady hastened to Elsa's side, he turned

away in silence, and passed out with bowed head through the door-way.

The morning had dawned dimly in the great room. The torches had burned out.

Love Motif

CHAPTER IV

HOW THE KNIGHT WENT AWAY

WHEN the King seated himself upon his throne, under the Oak of Justice, that morning, the sun, rising in majesty behind the hills, disclosed to him the Brabantian nobles assembled in full armor to await their leader, the Protector of Brabant. Soon the four nobles who had accompanied Telramund on the previous night appeared, bearing a bier, and announced that they had been sent to the King by the Protector of Brabant. At the same moment Elsa was seen advancing slowly, supported on either side by her ladies. Her robes were of many soft colors, embroidered with great richness and beauty, and the Brabantian circlet shone upon her fair hair; but her face was pale, and her sad eyes filled every heart with pity, for all fancied that she grieved because the hour drew near for her husband's departure for the wars. She was led to a lower throne, near that of the King, and sat there silent, and bowed with misery.

Then, amid a glad sound of welcome, the Protector of Brabant appeared, clad in the silver armor which he had worn at the time of his coming, with the same cloak hanging from his shoulders, the same golden horn gleaming at his belt, and his long sword at his side. Advancing to the King's throne, he sadly announced to him and to the assembled knights that he could not lead them to battle.

Checking the loud cries of dismay and wonder which greeted his words, he further said that he had a question to put to the people. He pointed to the bier borne by the four nobles, and after saying that Telramund had attempted his life unfairly, asked if he had been right in slaying him. All agreed that he had been but an instrument of God in dealing justice to a coward. Then, as the nobles bore the bier away in silence, the Knight, with solemn impressiveness, declared that his wife had been false to her word, that she had asked the questions which he had forbidden her, and from which she had promised him so earnestly to refrain. He was now prepared, he said, to answer her demands, and to tell all that he had concealed. Speaking in grave, hushed tones, the Knight began his tale.

"In a far land," he said, slowly, "stands a castle named Monsalvat. A shrine is within it, blessed by a marvellous Cup called the Holy Grail. The guardians of the sacred treasure are a great

Brotherhood of Knights, who are made strong with a might which conquers all evil. The Knights of the Brotherhood may journey to distant lands, on errands of mercy, help, or protection, and may continue to live among men ; but if they disclose the secret of their power they are forced to return to Monsalvat. I was sent as champion for the honor and rights of yonder lady, for I am one of the Brotherhood. The holy father of the Knights, and the holder of the crown of rulership, is Parsifal. I am his Knight, and I am named Lohengrin."

He ceased speaking. Many faces were wet with tears, and whispers of sorrow and awe were faintly heard from the people. Elsa started to her feet.

" The ground wavers beneath me," she muttered. " What darkness !"

" The swan !" cried the people, pointing to the gleaming river. " The swan—alas, he comes !"

" Horror ! The swan !" wailed Elsa, gazing with wide, terrified eyes at the glistening plumage of the bird, which was floating towards the shore on the bright undulations of the water.

" This is the summons of the Grail," said Lohengrin, sadly. " Oh, that this grief might have been spared us !"

The swan had now reached the shore, and the Knight addressed it in tones of regret :

" I had hoped that when the year was over

7

you might have sought me in your own shape."
He turned away, and going to Elsa's side bade her
farewell. There was no trace of reproach in his
words to her—only a deep and tender sorrow.

"Oh, Elsa!" he said. "When one year had
passed your brother would have been restored to
you through the Grail's might, for its power has
been shed upon him in protection. Now the condition has been forfeited; but if he ever comes home,
when I am dwelling far away, give him this horn,
this sword, and this ring. The horn will bring him
help on the battle-field, the sword will give him
victory in the fiercest combat, and seeing this ring
he will think of one who helped you in your
need."

One by one he put the gifts into Elsa's trembling
hands, and then, whispering with passionate tenderness, " Farewell, my wife, I return to the Grail!" he
turned hastily aside, and made his way to the edge
of the water.

Suddenly Ortrud, who had been standing in the
shadow of the King's throne, started forward, with
a loud peal of laughter.

" Pass homeward, valiant hero!" she cried, harshly; "you and your bride may now hear the truth.
I wound the chain about the neck of yonder swan
when I changed him from a boy to his present form.
He is the heir of Brabant!" She looked about her

defiantly, and as the knights in horror pressed forward about her she waved them back.

"Away from me!" she said, fiercely. "The gods have given me power for revenge—power which I can exercise upon you as well!"

With a look of wildness on her face, she stood silent—a lonely figure among many.

Lohengrin had heard her confession, and as she ceased he sank on his knees in prayer. Long he remained motionless, while all watched him in painful suspense. Suddenly a long beam of brilliant light streamed from the sky upon his upturned face, and down the shaft of brightness floated a snow-white dove, which sank with outstretched wings until it poised itself in the air above the boat. Quickly rising to his feet, Lohengrin unfastened the gold chain from the swan. The bird vanished under the ripple of the river, and in its place was a beautiful boy in garments of silver. Taking his hand, Lohengrin drew him onto the bank, and said, quietly, as he led him forward, "Behold the Duke of Brabant! To rule and lead you he has come!"

Gottfried bent in homage before the King, and, one and all, the Brabantians knelt, acknowledging their young ruler. Elsa caught him in her arms, in a transport of love and thankfulness. Ortrud sank prostrate across the step of the throne — a spirit of evil vanquished by good.

Lohengrin having swiftly entered the craft, the dove lifted the chain in its tiny beak, and drew the boat away. When Elsa raised her eyes from her brother's beloved face, she saw only the wave-broken, sparkling water, and darted forward with a sad cry: "My husband! my husband!"

Once more Lohengrin came in sight beyond a bend of the river. He leaned upon his shield and his head was bowed in sorrow. A loud cry of grief arose from the watchers, a cry echoing far over the clear waters. From Gottfried's loving embrace Elsa sank silently to the earth.

For the last time Lohengrin was seen in the far distance; then the many watching eyes saw only the change and gleam of the shining river—for he was gone.

Motif of the Holy Grail

TRISTAN AND ISOLDE

(*Tristan und Isolde*)

Motif of Tristan's Honor

Motif of the wounded Tristan, nursed by Isolde

CHAPTER I

FROM IRELAND TO CORNWALL

ONCE upon a time there was a Queen of Ireland named Isolde, who was well versed in the arts of sorcery, who could brew philters of marvellous magic powers, cure all sickness, subdue the sea to her will, and have calm or storm as she wished. She had a daughter, also named Isolde, who was extremely beautiful — tall and very fair, with hair of a deep brilliant gold, and clear, shining blue eyes. She inherited much of her mother's skill in caring for the sick, but none of her witchcraft, and her heart was so noble, compassionate, and generous that she was well-beloved by all.

The Queen of Ireland had a nephew, Morold by name, a knight of great courage, gigantic stature, and a nature in which pride, roughness, and cruelty were combined. To Sir Morold the Princess Isolde was betrothed. Every year the King of Ireland sent him to levy taxes on old Marke, the Cornish sovereign; for Cornwall, having been vanquished by Ireland, was obliged to pay weregild every year to the Irish people. Morold in his annual visits to King Marke made himself much feared and hated, for he was rude and insolent, and constantly taunted the old monarch about the taxes which he must pay to Ireland. The Cornish people grew more and more indignant, and finally Sir Tristan, King Marke's nephew, could no longer endure to hear the insults heaped upon Cornwall by a rough and heartless giant like Morold, and he challenged the Irish knight to mortal combat.

Tristan was the son of King Marke's sister, Blanchefleur, who had married the knight Rivalin, of Brittany, and had gone to dwell in his home, in far Kareol, by the sea. Rivalin had died not long after their marriage, and the Lady Blanchefleur, overcome by grief, died also, leaving a little son whom she had named Tristan (or Sadness). An old servitor, Kurvenal by name, took care of the boy, and carried him over the sea to his uncle, the monarch of Cornwall. The King had lost his wife long years before, and as he was without children of his own, and very lonely, he gladly welcomed his sister's child, brought him up as his son, and appointed him heir to the crown of Cornwall. The boy grew up strong and brave, and his exploits were known by all the world. Indeed, " Sir Tristan of Brittany " came to be a name significant of all courage, knight-liness, and nobility; and he it was who challenged Sir Morold of Ireland to combat.

Morold accepted the challenge, the day was appointed, and, with many anxious eyes upon them, the warriors met and fought for the freedom of Cornwall — the honor of Ireland. Morold, whose fierce soul was deeply angered, flung at his opponent a poisoned spear. It wounded Tristan severely, but before he fell he raised his good sword and killed the giant with one blow.

The Cornishmen, free once more, sent Morold's head home to Ireland with a derisive message, according to the ancient barbaric custom. It was delivered into the hands of the Princess Isolde, who discovered in it a splinter of steel, and vowed to seek through the world until she found the sword from which the piece had been broken. Then upon the bearer of that sword she would be revenged for the death of her kinsman and betrothed.

It was while the kingdom was still mourning the loss of Morold that a wounded harper appeared at the Irish court, sorely needing the care of the Queen and her daughter. Full of pity for all suffering, the two Isoldes welcomed the stranger, and the

Princess undertook to cure him by administering various of her mother's balsams and potions. Helped sometimes by her maid of honor, Brangäne, Isolde carefully nursed the harper—who called himself Tantris—until he began to recover slowly from his wound.

One day, while he slept, she sat near him, idly toying with his sword, which lay beside the couch. Suddenly she saw a notch in the blade, and, a horrible thought occurring to her, she hastened with the sword to the place where she kept the steel splinter concealed. When she found that the piece indeed fitted into the broken edge of the blade, she knew that the Tantris whom she had nursed was none other than the Tristan who had killed her kinsman, Morold. As she stood holding the sword in her hand the wounded knight called to her, and a wild wish to kill him with his own sword while he lay defenceless possessed her. Grasping the hilt, she went to the bedside and raised the sword. But, as though he saw neither uplifted arm nor poised weapon, he looked up tenderly and wonderingly into her eyes, and in a moment the thought of his weakness touched her burning heart. She lowered her hand, and let the sword drop to the floor.

From that hour she was untiring in her efforts to bring him back to health and strength. While all Ireland was in wild commotion, vowing death to

Morold's slayer, she guarded him in secrecy and security, refraining from a word which might draw suspicion upon him. And, as time went on, she found that she had grown to love the knight very dearly, and she believed that he loved her.

Then the day came for him to leave Ireland, and, promising to return, he sailed away. His mind was full of many new thoughts. His friends, alarmed at the seriousness of his wound, had urged him to go in disguise to the Irish Queen that she might cure him ; and though disguise or deceit in any form was most distasteful to his frank and brave nature, he had been persuaded to do as they wished as a last resort, that he might have hope of life and strength. And now he loved the Princess with his whole heart, though he did not know that she thought of him with anything save pity, and he dreaded her horror when she should learn his name.

He returned to the Cornish court and narrated his adventures. He spoke with such admiration and tenderness of the wonderful beauty and the generous heart of the Irish Princess that the court-iers and knights assured King Marke that there, in-deed, was a woman befitting the throne of Cornwall. The King, after much thought, decided to send to Ireland, requesting the hand of the Princess in mar-riage, and it was Tristan who was chosen for this task—who must carry his uncle's proposal and receive the answer, and, if consent were given, must bring Isolde to Cornwall. With a heavy heart, but sternly resolved to further the interests of his kinsman and benefactor in all things, Tristan sailed away to Ireland.

The suit of the King of Cornwall was accepted by the King and Queen of Ireland, and Tristan, in his uncle's name, declared peace between the two kingdoms. So, in the Irish court, before a great assembly of people, the feud was ended.

Only Isolde, furious, heart-broken, despairing, did not join in the general declaration of friendliness, but repented that she had spared the life of this knight, who had won her love and now dared to woo her for his uncle, the King. And the horror of it all caused her to fall almost distraught with misery. As though frozen with a grief too deep for outward sign, she allowed all to be made ready for her departure. She bade farewell to her parents with neither tears nor smiles, and silently went on board Sir Tristan's ship.

Queen Isolde, distressed at her daughter's strange state of mind, intrusted to Brangäne, who was to accompany the Princess, a casket of magic philters—the most valuable gift she could bestow. A love-potion was among these, and the Queen directed Brangäne to give it to Isolde and King Marke on their wedding-day, to insure their mutual love and happiness.

Promising to obey these instructions, the maid of honor followed her young mistress to the ship, which weighed anchor and sailed away from Ireland.

Much sorrow went with the vessel, for Isolde believed that the knight did not love her, and that he willingly relinquished her to the King; and Tristan, firm in his decision to be true to his uncle, suffered in silence, loving Isolde deeply, but having this consolation—the belief that she had no love for him, and, therefore, did not suffer as did he. So the ship sailed on to Cornwall.

The Melody of the Sailor's Song
(Also used as the Sea Motif)

The last day of the voyage dawned bright and fair. A warm wind blew freshly; the waves of the blue sea rolled with rhythmical music against the sides of the vessel; sunshine lay upon everything; a blue line on the western horizon showed that port would soon be gained.

A flight of steps led from Isolde's cabin to a part of the deck which had been curtained off for her and transformed by a canopy into a sort of pavilion. It was richly hung with tapestries, and upon a raised dais stood a couch covered with furs and costly draperies. Upon a stand was a golden flagon of wine and a goblet.

Isolde, silent and brooding, lay upon the couch, with her face buried among the soft cushions and her hands clasped above her head. Brangäne stood at the side of the ship, looking off to the west, where land lay, a blue stripe against the sky. From the rigging above came the sound of a sailor's voice singing. The clear tones were wafted to them on the boisterous sea-wind, and aroused Isolde from her apathy. Turning to Brangäne, she asked, as though in a dream, whither they were sailing. Brangäne answered that they would soon be in Cornwall, and Isolde sprang up, declaring, in furious excitement, that she wished never to reach Cornwall, and passionately regretting that she had not her mother's power over wind and wave. As though in a wild hope that sorcery lurked somewhere in her own heart, she appealed to the breezes then blowing, bidding them arise and become tempestuous blasts, and wreck the ship in the surging ocean.

As Brangäne, much startled by this outburst, hastened near with words of anxiety and wonder, Isolde pushed her away and sank upon the couch, crying, "Air! Air!"

Brangäne quickly drew back the curtains, revealing the length of the ship. Sailors sat and stood about the deck, coiling ropes or talking together. Various knights who had accompanied Tristan sat in the stern of the ship, and near them, though apart, was Tristan, standing motionless, with eyes which seemed to gaze out unseeing over the restless, changing waves.

He was in half-armor, with a long cloak about him, and his strong, bare arms were encircled by metal bands. In his helmet were the wings of some white bird, and his sword hung at his side, in a scabbard covered with intricate designs. An imposing and knightly figure was his, but Isolde's eyes rested on his face. It was naturally fair, but deeply tanned by the sun, and his head was covered with short, curling brown hair. His eyes, steadfast and clear, seemed saddened by an unseen shadow which lay within them—the shadow cast, perhaps, by fate—the shadow that lingered about his name, Sadness.

For some time Isolde watched him, while strange and conflicting thoughts passed through her mind. Suddenly she laughed, with odd mockery.

" What think you of him ?" she said to Brangäne, who, rather bewildered, asked to whom she referred.

"That hero !" returned Isolde. " He who fears to meet my eyes !"

" Do you mean Sir Tristan, my lady ?" exclaimed Brangäne. " The wonder of the world — the hero worthy of all honor ?"

"Shrinking and shamed, he brings the bride," declared Isolde, scornfully. "Trying to hide his embarrassment as he carries her to his King! Go!" she cried, imperatively—"Go ask him if he dares to come to me! He has persistently neglected me on the voyage—see if he has courage to face me!"

"Shall I beseech him to attend you?" questioned the maid.

But Isolde answered, haughtily, "No! Command him! It is the Princess who speaks—I, Isolde!"

Very unwillingly Brangäne walked down the deck between the lines of sailors to Tristan.

"Have a care!" muttered Kurvenal, pulling his young master's cloak. "Here is word from Isolde."

Tristan started, murmuring "Isolde!" and turned towards the maid, saying, quietly, "What message does my lady send me?"

Brangäne bent low before him as she answered. She asked him, respectfully, to go to her mistress, who desired to speak with him. Tristan inquired if the Lady Isolde were very tired with the voyage, and assured her that they would reach land before sunset. When Brangäne nervously repeated her mistress's request, Tristan said, gently, that he would go to the Princess when the time came for him to lead her before the King.

"My Lord Tristan," besought the maid, at a loss

how to appeal to this obdurate knight, "my lady
wished you to attend her at once !"

" I have but one wish—to serve her," said Tristan,
seemingly unmoved. " If I left the helm, how could
I know that the ship were well steered to King
Marke's domain ?"

" Sir Tristan, is it possible that you do not understand me?" cried Brangäne. " Listen, now ! Thus
has my lady spoken : ' Command him ! It is the
Princess who speaks—I, Isolde !' "

At this point Kurvenal sprang to his feet and
broke out into words of rude contempt for the Lady
Isolde's will, and finally sang a rough song about
the slaying of Morold, which was taken up loudly
by the sailors. Brangäne hastily made her way back
to her mistress, closing the curtains behind her, and
sank on her knees before the couch. Isolde had
heard Kurvenal's scoffing song, and her heart was
sore with rage and humiliation. Starting up, as Brangäne described her interview with Tristan, she interrupted her, and cried that if she willed she could
put an end to such mockery and slights. Beckoning
Brangäne to approach nearer, she told her, in a low
voice, the story of the stranger who had come to
Ireland, whom she had nursed and discovered to be
a foe, whom she would have killed save for a momentary weakness.

" How wonderful !" exclaimed Brangäne, softly.

8

"The knight I sometimes helped you nurse! Why
have I not recognized him?"

Then, as Isolde declared wildly that she should
never cease to regret that her foolish pity had prevented her from letting the blade descend into his
heart, Brangäne gently endeavored to soothe and
calm her, trying all forms of tenderness, cajolery,
and reason to comfort her mistress's sad heart. To
convince her of her future happiness with King
Marke, the maid then told her of the casket intrusted to her by the Queen of Ireland. As Isolde bade
her bring the magic philters, Brangäne hastened
away, returning in a few moments with a golden
casket. She knelt beside Isolde, who seated herself
upon the couch and raised the lid, disclosing rows
of tiny phials.

"Here," she said, "are potions of all kinds. Here
is a salve which cures sickness and soothes wounds;
here are antidotes for all poisons. And here is the
best and most helpful draught for you!" She took
out a bottle—the love-potion.

"Nay," said Isolde, quietly, and put out her hand,
touching one of the flasks. "I marked this once,
that I might know it. This is the one which I would
drink."

"The death-draught!" shrieked Brangäne, starting back.

Isolde rose to her feet, the flask of death in her

hand. From without the curtains came the cries of the sailors. The end of the journey was almost reached. Kurvenal pushed the curtains aside and entered, saying that it was his master's request that the ladies should hasten, as already King Marke's castle was visible, and Sir Tristan was ready to escort the Princess to the shore. In answer, Isolde said that she would neither hasten nor prepare to land until Tristan had come in person to apologize for his past misdeeds. With a defiant gesture Kurvenal left them, and Isolde, in intense excitement, turned to Brangäne and bade her prepare the draught of peace. "You know how to make it," she added, significantly. And as Brangäne still seemed bewildered, she showed her the death-potion, bidding her pour it into the golden goblet. In that draught, declared the Princess, she and Tristan would drink everlasting truce.

Falling at Isolde's feet, the maid besought her to have mercy—not to command so horrible a task.

"Will you not be true to me?" asked Isolde, grasping her arm as the terrified woman raised it appealingly.

"Oh, misery!" wailed Brangäne, cowering before her.

"Sir Tristan!" announced Kurvenal, parting the curtains.

Isolde walked quietly to the couch and supported herself by resting her hand upon its head.

" Sir Tristan may approach," she said, gravely, and with dignity.

Tristan entered slowly, pausing with lowered head before letting the curtains close behind him. With deep respect, he asked what was her will with him, and when Isolde demanded the cause of his neglect during the voyage, he said, tranquilly, that it was the custom in his land that a deputy bringing a bride to her future husband should in courtesy to her refrain from intruding upon her while on the journey. Isolde, with much scorn, told him that he would do well to remember other customs — truce with foes, and amends for base deeds.

" What foes?" asked Tristan.

"Question your own fear!" returned Isolde, bitterly and mockingly. " There is blood-guilt between us!"

And when he declared that the feud had been healed, she cried, sharply, " Not between us ! I was silent in the truce !"

Then she reminded him of the days when she had so carefully concealed him from suspicious hearts and murderous hands, when she had restrained the impulse which prompted her to slay him, and she declared, passionately, that were Morold alive all would be well, and she should not have to punish her enemies herself.

Tristan had grown pale with intense feeling as she spoke, and with a sudden, fierce, hurt gesture he drew his sword and offered it to her, bidding her slay him now, since she so deeply mourned Morold's death and so greatly repented her momentary soft-ness of heart when she held that same hilt before. Isolde answered that King Marke would be angry if she killed his nephew and messenger, and said that she would declare a truce if Tristan would drink with her the customary draught of peace. Turning to Brangäne, she commanded her to pre-pare the concoction of which she had spoken. The maid, pale and trembling, advanced to the stand and opened the casket. From without came the sound of the sailor's " Yo-heave-ho!" Tristan started from the deep reverie into which he had fallen, cry-ing, " Where are we?"

" Near the end," said Isolde, darkly. " Tristan, is the feud healed?"

Brangäne handed her the filled goblet, and, with it in her hand, Isolde went towards Tristan, who stood silent, looking into her eyes.

The shouts of the men were louder, more boister-ous. " Anchor down!" they cried.

Tristan had known from the beginning of the in-terview that Isolde wished his death. He now took the goblet from her and spoke in accents of deep and strange yearning : " I thank you for this draught.

In return I give you my oath of truce—Tristan's
honor—highest truth! Tristan's pain—bravest suffering! Drink of death, I take you gladly!" He raised
the goblet to his lips and drank. Isolde snatched it
from his hand and swallowed the remainder of the
potion. There was a pause. The golden goblet
fell from her hand and rolled along the deck unnoticed.

Tristan and Isolde stood motionless with beating
hearts, and eyes in which dawned a new and strange
emotion. They trembled, and then bent their heads
as though against a strong wind ; then turning to
one another, each spoke the other's name, wonderingly, as in a dream. In a moment they were in
each other's arms.

" Hail, King Marke ! Hail !" shouted the sailors
outside. Brangäne wrung her hands wildly and despairingly, looking at her mistress and the knight in
horror ; for, overcome by fear of the consequences,
she had prepared not the death-draught but another.
Now she regretted the deception which had been
intended for the Princess's welfare, and which, the
maid now realized, would undoubtedly cause the
deepest distress to all.

The curtains were drawn back ; the ship was in
port. On the rocks could be seen a great castle.
Brangäne called down the hatchway to Isolde's
women, who appeared with the crown and royal

robe which she, the Princess of Ireland, must wear when she should meet the King. Brangäne hastily put the crown upon her mistress's head and wrapped the mantle about her. Kurvenal rushed in, announcing the coming of King Marke in a small bark to meet his bride.

"Brangäne!" gasped Isolde, clinging to her maid of honor; "what was that draught?"

"The love-potion!" moaned Brangäne, pushing her forward.

Tristan took her hand, and, supported by him and her women, Isolde, weak and overpowered, was led forward to meet the King.

Love Motif

CHAPTER II

IN ISOLDE'S GARDEN

THE time drew near for Isolde to wed the King. Marke, a gentle and generous man, was filled with love for the beautiful woman who so soon would be his bride, and treated her with all the honor which he could have accorded her had she been already Queen of Cornwall and he her vassal. She was allotted the grandest apartments of the castle, her own room opening out into a beautiful garden which bordered on a dense, shadowy forest. So she dwelt in peace and luxury with Brangäne and her attendants; the days passed, and the wedding-tide was near.

King Marke's knights were delighted with the Irish Princess. One and all had been much touched by her weakness on the day of her arrival, for every one attributed it to a hard voyage. All Cornwall prepared to serve the pale and lovely lady most faithfully when she should be Queen.

Only one knight felt aught save honor and homage in his heart, and that was Sir Melot, a man of hot and wayward impulses, sometimes generous, sometimes treacherous, always ambitious. Tristan had long counted him his truest and best friend, and Marke, too, had depended greatly upon him during Tristan's absence, and trusted him absolutely. Two motives now worked havoc in Melot's heart. A desire to be first in Marke's love and confidence had long been growing within him, and by degrees a wish to see Tristan expelled from favor had taken definite form. Now, moreover, the beautiful face of the Princess Isolde had awakened love in his heart, and he grew sullen and gloomy, knowing the hopelessness of aspiring to her hand. On the ship his sharp eyes had seen her pallor—had seen, too, how dazed and unnatural Tristan had seemed. He drew swift conclusions, and decided that the Princess had given the King's nephew and messenger her love. This thought became clearer as the days passed, and his jealousy of Tristan grew to hatred, and he found himself creeping stealthily about, like one seeking to pass unnoticed. His mind gave itself up to plotting, and several times Brangäne found him in dim corners, listening. Much disgusted, she formed her own opinion of his deceitful appearance, and distrusted and detested him with all her heart. So one day, when she heard that King Marke and his court were going on a hunt that night, she decided to be particularly watchful.

Isolde waited impatiently for dusk and the departure of the hunting-party. At a signal from her, Tristan was to meet her in the garden and they were to have a long talk together. The glamour of the magic love - potion was still about them, and they had scarcely thought of the outside world since that last day on the ship. Isolde forgot that she was going to be married to King Marke, and Tristan thought no more of either self-sacrifice or fealty to his uncle.

The love-potion, while it had not influenced their love, which had been too deep before to be increased, had shut out the memory of everything external, so that now they thought only of each other.

Twilight came, and deepened into night. The hunting - party started and rode off through the woods, with a loud sound of horns and the general excitement attendant upon the chase. Brangäne hastened out onto the stone steps which led from her mistress's chamber into the garden, and stood listening to the retreating horns.

The shadows lay dim on the grass; the wind stirred the leaves of the forest trees. In the garden was a high bank covered with flowers, which gave a fresh, sweet fragrance to the night breezes. Far and farther away sounded the horns, blending musically with the whisper of the trees, the soft sigh of the wind, and the light ripple of a fountain hidden in the dusky shrubbery.

"Can you still hear the horns?" asked Isolde, coming eagerly to the door. She had flung a soft white veil over her head, and stood, a tall, queenly figure in trailing snowy robes, outlined against the darkness of her unlighted room. Just at the doorway a torch was fastened in a niche, and the brightness fell softly upon the two women, and dimly showed a long flight of steps near them, which led up, on the outside of the castle, to a watch-tower above Isolde's apartments.

There was a pause after the Princess had spoken. Softly, like an echo, came the far-off horn-calls to Brangäne's attentive ears. She nodded her head and answered in a low voice, " I still hear them— quite plainly."

Isolde came to her side and listened for a moment. " You are too anxious," she said ; "you are deluded by the leaves that softly murmur, answering the laughing wind !"

Brangäne declared that indeed she heard the horns, and besought her mistress to beware of him who planned the night-hunt, for she suspected treachery. Isolde replied that Sir Melot, Tristan's friend, had planned it, and she resolutely refused to listen to Brangäne's earnest warnings against the knight. She commanded the maid to put out the torch, for that was the signal which would bring Tristan to her. Almost frantic with apprehension, Brangäne entreated her not to have the torch extinguished that night, and sorrowfully bewailed her folly in mixing so fatal a draught. But Isolde was too impatient to heed her words, and directed her to mount the steps, keep a keen lookout from the watch-tower, and let them know if spies or enemies drew near.

Reluctant, but always obedient, Brangäne ascended the stairs and stationed herself in the tower, whence she could watch the forest-path and all other approaches to the castle.

Isolde had removed the torch from the niche, and now threw it to the ground, where the flame died out. Then she hastened to the staircase, and mounted a few steps that she might see farther. At last she perceived a dark figure approaching swiftly, and she tore off her veil, waving it eagerly. Then flinging it from her, she sprang forward to meet Tristan.

After their first glad words of greeting they began to talk of the past, when they had first known and loved each other. Isolde accused Tristan gently of forgetting her for a time, but he explained to her that his heart had been filled with the glory of her

beauty and her nobility when he seemed most indifferent, and that he had felt only too deeply the misery of fate when he was obliged to woo her for another. And Isolde told him the reasons for all her bitterness and scorn—her love and wounded pride, which made her seem harsh and mocking even while her heart was breaking. So they continued to talk, satisfying themselves and each other with assurances and proofs of their love and fidelity.

Then, with the magic of the night about them—a spell gentler though scarcely less strong than the potent love-draught—they seated themselves upon the bank of flowers, and spoke in whispers, addressing the quiet, sheltering night, which gave them rest and contentment, and for their happiness studded the deep sky with softly gleaming stars. For they fancifully pretended that all night's beauties had been made for them, and were revealed to them alone, for those few hours. Perhaps they unconsciously felt that the end of the dream was near, and that they must catch the glamour ere it passed into the light of day.

Suddenly they heard Brangäne, in the watchtower above them, singing a watch-song, warningly, fearfully:

> " Lonely watch I through the night,
> You, in fancies of love-light,
> This my call, oh ! heed aright !

> All your joy must swiftly cease,
> Grief will startle soon your peace.
> Heed and hark!
> Heed and hark!
> Soon will pass the dark!"

"Listen," said Isolde. "The day will come, and we must part."

"The day has not yet come," returned Tristan, dreamily. And again they began to talk, more sorrowfully now, for the sense of foreboding was heavy upon both, and when Tristan said, gently, that it would be well if they could pass out of earthly life together, Isolde silently assented, and bowed her head, overcome with emotion. Once more came the warning voice from the watch-tower:

> ' Heed and hark!
> Heed and hark!
> Day soon speeds the dark!"

Rising from the bank of flowers, they tried to forget the boding sorrow of the call in eager, passionate words of love and hope. Suddenly a wild shriek sounded from the watch-tower, and Brangäne hurried down the turret stairs to her mistress's side. Kurvenal hastened from the wood, begging Tristan to save himself. Isolde sank down upon the bank as King Marke and his knights, led by Melot, entered the garden.

The King stood as though overpowered with amazement and pain. Tristan met the curious and wondering eyes of all as though in a dream.

The day dawned. Long red beams of light shone between the dark trunks of the forest trees, and the garden and all within it were illumined by the radiance.

"Now was I not right, my King?" demanded Melot, harshly, leaning on his sword. "Did I not tell you that Tristan had forgotten to be true to you?"

Old King Marke was bowed with grief. He looked at his nephew in wondering pain while he spoke in low, broken tones of the sorrow which this shock caused him, of the tenderness in his heart inspired by the sweet Irish princess, and the unquestioning trust which he had always felt for Tristan. Gently, though with inexpressible sadness, he asked the young knight to explain everything to him—to tell him the whole story frankly.

Tristan, who had seemed in a trance, was half aroused by the sorrow in the King's voice, and raised his eyes pitifully to his. But he answered, vaguely, "Ah, King, I cannot tell you—nothing can be answered."

Then he turned to Isolde, and told her gently that he was going upon a long journey into a strange, shadowy land, and asked her if she wished

to follow him.   She answered, gravely and softly,
that wherever he went she would follow, for she
loved him and would remain true to him forever.

Melot rushed forward with drawn sword, crying
to Tristan, " You are a traitor!"   Tristan turned
quickly towards him, looking at him with a scorn
which made the knight flinch.

" This was my friend," said Tristan, contemptuously.   " He assured me of his affection and faith-
fulness.   He upheld my fame, he flattered me, and
—betrayed me!   On guard, Melot!" and he drew
his sword.

Melot sprang forward.   As he struck at Tristan
the latter lowered his blade, allowing himself to be
wounded.   King Marke dragged Melot back and
forcibly withheld him from moving.   Kurvenal
caught his master in his arms, and Isolde rushed to
his side in agonized horror.

Upon the old King's face was now a deep sorrow, before which even Melot was silent.

Motif of King Marke

CHAPTER III

KAREOL

KURVENAL carried Tristan to the shore, and set sail at once for Kareol, where Rivalin's ancestral castle stood. There he nursed his young master tenderly, trusting at first that time, care, and rest might restore his health. Then, as the knight grew no stronger, the faithful old servitor, after long thought, despatched Tristan's ship to Cornwall with an appeal to the Lady Isolde to come to Brittany, that her tenderness and well-known skill might cure his master of his wound.

On the day when he hoped for the ship's return he carried Tristan into the castle court-yard, and laid him upon a couch which he had prepared under a spreading lime-tree. He seated himself to watch and wait beside the knight, who lay in an unbroken stupor. Only his faint breathing told Kurvenal that he still lived, and the old man sat looking sadly and tenderly on the white, wasted face of his beloved master.

9

The court-yard had been neglected for many years, and it was overgrown by low green weeds and vines, and strewn with broken rocks. The castle originally had been a magnificent one, with a watch-tower, battlements, a large gate, and all the ancient means of defence. Now the tower was dilapidated, the battlements broken in places, and the gate accessible to friend or foe. A lonely and dreary spot was Tristan's home in Kareol; but Kurvenal, as he turned his eyes from the knight's face to the wide, far-stretching sea, did not think of the desolate outlook, but only wondered, in an agony of doubt and fear, if Isolde would come that day to bring Tristan back to life. Kurvenal had posted a shepherd on the rocks below the castle, bidding him play a sad melody on his pipe while he saw no ship upon the sea, and a merry one when a sail became visible. The monotonous music of the pipe came drearily to Kurvenal's anxious ears, signifying the empty sea.

Finally the shepherd ceased to play, and climbing the rocks to the battlements, looked over and cried, in a hushed voice, "Kurvenal! Does our lord still sleep?"

" If he wakes," returned Kurvenal, mournfully, " I fear it will be for the last time, unless the lady comes. Is there no ship in sight?"

The shepherd shook his head as he turned away.

"I should play another tune if there were." He shaded his eyes with his hand, looking off towards the ocean. "Blank and desolate is the sea," he said, and slowly clambered down the rocks.

In a moment the melody of his pipe sounded again. Tristan, stirring weakly, heard it, and recognizing the notes which had often penetrated his stupor, muttered, faintly, "The old tune! Why does it wake me?"

"Ah! It is his voice!" exclaimed Kurvenal, bending over him. "Tristan! Master! My lord!"

The knight's voice came again, very feebly: "Who speaks to me? Kurvenal, you? Where am I?"

"At home, in Kareol," answered Kurvenal, delightedly, "where you will rest and grow strong again!"

Raising himself with difficulty, Tristan tried to tell the strange dreams and shadows which had haunted him during his illness, the marvellous lands which he had seen, the darkness, the mist; and as he spoke he drifted off once more to half-conscious delirium, and spoke of the light which seemed to surround Isolde, and finally, his voice growing fainter, of the torch, for the extinguishing of which he fancied that he was waiting. He sank into a stupor once more, but Kurvenal endeavored eagerly to arouse him by speaking of Isolde, and assuring the knight that she was even then on her way to him.

At first the words could not pierce the dim shadows and fancies of the sick man's brain, but at last he understood, and embraced his old servant in wild gratitude.

Delirium seized him once more. He raised himself upon his knee on the couch, and fancying that he saw the ship that bore Isolde, hailed it in a voice to which fever had given an unnatural power. Even as he gazed, panting, upon the blank, blue sea, the melancholy music of the shepherd's pipe sounded from the rocks below, and Kurvenal explained sadly that the ship was not yet to be seen.

" Is that its meaning?" questioned Tristan, wearily, as he sank back. " Is that the meaning of that old, hopeless melody's mournful notes?" He lapsed into unconsciousness. A few minutes passed, during which Kurvenal listened anxiously for his heart-beats; at last the knight whispered, " The ship—do you see it yet?"

" The ship?" repeated Kurvenal, with forced cheerfulness. " It must soon be here."

Tristan slowly lifted his head and supported himself on his arm, while a dreamy light came into his eyes. Wistfully, tenderly he spoke :

"On board is Isolde, smiling as she bears the drink of truce. Do you not see her? Lifted on waves of loveliest flowers she lightly floats to land. Her smile gives me trust and rest, her touch brings healing and comfort. Ah, Isolde, how beautiful you are !" Then, growing suddenly excited, he raised himself higher, for a vision was revealed to him. " Kurvenal, go and watch ! I see so clearly, you also must see it ! Hasten ! Hasten !" He trembled with frantic agitation, pointing wildly—" The ship ! The ship ! Do you not see it ?"

At the same moment a merry tune was heard coming from the rocks below. Faster and faster played the shepherd, telling that the sail was in sight. Kurvenal rushed up into the watch-tower.

There, indeed, was the ship, speeding to the shore. As she came nearer, he called joyfully down to Tristan, describing the approach, the coming into harbor, the scarf which he could see being waved from the deck, the arrival at the strand, the eager spring with which Isolde came on shore.

"Away !" cried Tristan. " Help her—help my dear lady !"

Bidding him be calm and patient, Kurvenal hastened away to meet Isolde.

The suspense and sudden relief had been too great for Tristan's weakness. His delirium returned and he sprang up in mad excitement. Unconscious of his own acts, he tore the bandages from his wound and staggered from the couch to the centre of the court-yard.

"She is near!" he cried, wildly. "She who will help me and ease my pain!"

From without came Isolde's voice, full of love and hope, calling, "Tristan!"

His mind was wandering; he fancied himself once more in the dark woods waiting for her signal that he might hasten to her. He gazed, unseeing, in the direction of the voice.

"What is it — the light?" he muttered, gasping for breath. "The torchlight! Ah! the torch is out! I come! I come!"

The great gate swung open and Isolde hastened into the court-yard. She caught him in her arms as with unsteady steps he tried to meet her, supporting him, as he sank to the stone floor without strength to do aught save lift his hand feebly towards hers.

"Tristan!" whispered Isolde, staring wonderingly and fearfully at his face.

"Isolde!" answered Tristan, softly, and then was silent. And in that moment, indeed, the torch died out.

Isolde bent over him, trying to arouse him by tender words, but at last her strength left her and she sank down unconscious beside him. Kurvenal had followed her and now stood motionless, gazing upon his master's face.

From the harbor came the sound of voices and the

clang of armor. The shepherd and the steersman of the ship which had brought Isolde hastened into the court-yard, crying that another vessel had come fast behind Tristan's, and that even now armed men were landing in great numbers. Kurvenal, who had seemed petrified, roused himself and gazed off over the ramparts to the shore. When he saw King Marke and his warriors he commenced, with the aid of the two men, to bar the broken gate. Then crying that he would die before allowing any one to enter, he grasped his sword firmly, and took his stand inside the gateway with mingled determination, fierceness, and exaltation in his face.

Brangäne's voice was heard calling wildly, "Isolde, mistress!"

"What do you seek here?" demanded Kurvenal.

"Unbar the gate, Kurvenal!" cried Brangäne. "Where is Isolde?"

"You are false to her," returned Kurvenal, loudly; "you come with foes!"

At this point Melot appeared at the gateway with a force of warriors. "Away, you fool!" he exclaimed. "Do not try to resist!"

Kurvenal laughed bitterly.

"Hail to the day when I greet you!" he shouted, savagely, and darted towards the knight, striking at him with his sword. As Melot fell, mortally wounded, he saw the motionless figures of Tristan and Isolde within the court-yard, and moaning, "Alas, Tristan!" he died.

"Kurvenal, you are mistaken. Hold!" cried Brangäne, despairingly. For all answer, Kurvenal, who was now beside himself with excitement and fury, sprang forward, battling fiercely with the men-at-arms. Marke's voice, commanding him to cease, only caused him to rush upon the King himself. Meanwhile Brangäne had succeeded in climbing up the rocks and over the battlements, and now hastened to Isolde's side, wailing, "Mistress! Ah, Isolde, are you living?"

Kurvenal, driven back and fatally wounded, made his way to where Tristan lay, and sank lifeless at his feet. Marke, following quickly, gazed down in profound grief at his dearly loved knight and nephew, and at the woman who might have been his own wife.

Brangäne, sobbing, attempted to revive the Princess. The maid's heart was almost broken, for, in the hope of setting all right at last, she had confessed the story of the love-potion to the good King. He had instantly set sail to assure Tristan and Isolde of his belief in them and his comprehension of all that they had suffered, and, moreover, to unite them forever in token of his love. And now it was too late.

Tenderly raising Isolde's head on her arm, Bran-

"FROM HER LIPS CAME SOFTLY HER HEART'S SPEECH IN WORDS"

gäne told the King that her mistress still lived, and then besought her to listen to their explanations. But Isolde seemed neither to see nor to hear.

In deep and tender sorrow King Marke spoke to her, attempting to recall her to life and sense. But she remained lying with her head upon Brangäne's knee, alive, but as though in a strange trance.

" Hear you not?" questioned Brangäne, gently. " Isolde, dearest! Can you not believe the truth?"

Isolde rose slowly from the maid's supporting arms and gazed down upon her knight in deep, quiet happiness. She felt that she was surrounded by winds of marvellous music, by clear tones of gladness, by waves of radiance—growing, swelling, surging about her, until from her lips came softly her heart's speech in words. Describing the glorious things which she heard and saw, her happiness rose to an exaltation unearthly in its height. Swift and more swiftly whirled the light about her, great winds seemed to bear her soul on their might, music unspeakably sublime enveloped her spirit, and at last, whispering, " The highest happiness!" she sank lifeless upon the knight's body.

Pure and bright in the west was the sunset glory, shining softly across the sea into the stone courtyard at Kareol.

The King, as he raised his hands in a tender blessing over Tristan and Isolde, seemed to hear

around him music which rose in ethereal ascension
and was lost in the high clouds—music that seemed
to celebrate some union in the far, strange land to
which they had wished to go—music that rose in
marvellous, impalpable harmonies, voicing the highest happiness.

Motif of the Death of Tristan and Isolde

THE MASTERSINGERS OF NUREMBERG

(Die Meistersinger)

CHAPTER I

TRIAL BY THE MASTERS

IN the middle of the sixteenth century the sleepy old town of Nuremberg was considered by its inhabitants an art centre of no small importance. The good burghers had formed a guild devoted to the cultivation and exposition of the Art of Song, and the members of this guild were called Mastersingers. Every man who wished to enter it was obliged to compose a song according to the rules of the guild, and to sing it in correct time and tune. If the masters approved his performance, he was installed as one of the Mastersingers of Nuremberg.

The guild at the time of the beginning of this story was composed of twelve members, all good singers and excellent townsmen: Hans Sachs, the generous cobbler, who had been a widower for

many years, but was none the less genial for that,
and who might have boasted, had he wished, of the
greatest skill in singing and in shoemaking of any
man in Nuremberg; Veit Pogner, the goldsmith, a
widower, too, and though neither so kindly nor so
genial as his friend and neighbor Sachs, yet an up-
right, justly honored man, whose beautiful daughter
was the pet and pride of the townspeople; Kunz
Vogelgesang, the furrier; Conrad Nachtigall, the
buckle-maker; Sixtus Beckmesser, the town-clerk,
a withered, solemn little man, small in mind and
spiteful at heart; Balthazar Zorn, the pewterer;
Fritz Kothner, the baker; Ulric Eisslinger, the
grocer; Augustin Moser, the tailor; Hermann Or-
tell, the soap-boiler; Hans Schwartz, the stocking-
weaver; Hans Foltz, the coppersmith; these were
the Mastersingers of Nuremberg. Every one had
a boy apprenticed to him, to whom he taught the
Art of Song, together with his special branch of
trade. All these good men did their best to become skilled workmen and great Mastersingers, and
all were just and unflinching in their duty—all, that
is to say, except Beckmesser, the town-clerk, of
whom no one expected anything save selfishness,
envy, and dishonesty.

One summer, a young Franconian knight, named
Walther von Stolzing, made his appearance in Nuremberg, with a letter of introduction to Veit Pogner

from a friend. The goldsmith welcomed him to his house, and there the courteous manner, handsome face, and poetical speech of the new-comer awoke in the heart of Pogner's daughter, light-hearted Eva, a feeling entirely new and strange; for this knight was very unlike her own grave and good father, or the cringing, crafty Beckmesser, or even the kind cobbler who had played with her when she was a little child and sat on his knee. And the knight felt his heart thrill as he watched Eva's bright eyes and arch smiles, and heard her sweet, clear voice echoing through Pogner's old house.

Eva's life had been contented and free from all changes or excitement. Owing to a greater degree of wealth and culture than his neighbors, her father kept somewhat aloof from the rude burghers, and she had no companions save him, Hans Sachs, and her maid, Magdalene (or Lene). So she grew up, like a bird whose wings beat the air of a small sheltered valley, happy in a limitation which it does not recognize. Though she was gentle at heart, Eva's childlike love of fun often led her to tease those about her unmercifully, and a strain of coquetry gave her numberless airs and graces which nevertheless did not hide her real sweetness and tenderness. Her character was in reality that of a child, though Veit Pogner, even then, was considering the advisability of finding a husband for her.

The good man cared for but one thing more than
his daughter, and that was his art—Nuremberg's art
—German art—the art for which, according to his
views, any man should be glad to give all that he
had.   An idea occurred to him, a plan by which he
could help this art and make his daughter happy.
The time was approaching for the great song festival held every year in the meadows near Nuremberg.   At that time there would be a competition in
singing, and to the master who could best sing the
most correctly composed song would be awarded
the prize—this was the custom.   Now Veit Pogner
decided to offer Eva's hand in marriage to the winner, the only condition being that she herself should
be satisfied with the man.   The goldsmith was determined upon one thing—she must be the wife of
a mastersinger only—none save a follower of art
should wed her.

One morning, after the arrival of Sir Walther von
Stolzing, Eva and Magdalene went to service in
St. Katherine's Church.   Walther stationed himself
at a point whence he could watch Eva's bent head,
with its rippling, golden-brown hair falling in two
loose braids and half covered by a small white
cap.

It was the morning of St. John's Eve, and the people sang a slow, beautiful choral, voices and organ
combining in solemn harmonies:

"THE KNIGHT HAD JUST BESOUGHT EVA TO REPLY"

" Unto thee the Saviour came,
   To receive baptismal name.
   Hope of pardon gave He thus ;
   Ere His sacrifice for us.
   Came we for sacrament to thee,
   Worthier His death were we.
   Saint and leader,
   Christ's preceder,
   Lead us, as we go
   Forth on Jordan's flow."

The organ ceased, the service was over, and the people filed out of the church. Eva and Magdalene, who were among the last to depart, were stopped by Walther, who besought Eva to answer him one question, and thus set his heart at rest. Eva, anxious to talk to the knight without Magdalene's curious eyes upon her, sent the maid back to her seat first for a kerchief and then for a scarf-pin which she had dropped. Meanwhile, Walther had time to ask her the question—her answer to which would mean so much to him, he declared—" Are you betrothed?"

When Magdalene returned for the last time the knight had just besought Eva to reply. Greeting him with a courtesy, the maid noticed his agitation, and looked at him with distrust. Seeing that she did not understand the cause of his perturbation, Eva said, quickly and gently, making use of the soft

10

German diminutive, " Good Lenchen, he only wishes
to know—how can I explain? He asks—if I am betrothed !"

At this point a young fellow in the garb of an
apprentice entered, and proceeded to draw two curtains, shutting off the part of the church in which
they were standing from the rest of the building.
Lene's rosy face expressed delight, and she called
" David !" in a whisper.

Upon Eva's beseeching her to answer the knight
for her, the maid turned reluctantly from David and
said, with some severity, " Sir Knight, it is very dif-
ficult to reply to your question.   Eva Pogner is undoubtedly betrothed."

" But the bridegroom is unknown !" declared Eva,
eagerly.

" The bridegroom will be known to-morrow, when
the prize is given to the mastersinger," proceeded
Magdalene.

And Eva again interrupted her, softly, " And I,
his bride, will give him his wreath of victory !"

" Mastersinger ?" repeated the knight, amazed.

" You are not one ?" questioned Eva, with timid
disappointment.

" Is it to be a song trial?" asked Walther.

" Before the judges !" answered Magdalene.

" The prize," he began, vaguely, and with bewilder-
ment, " is won by—"

" Him whom the masters approve," replied the maid, with decision.

" The bride, then, will choose—"

"You or no one!" cried Eva, forgetting everything except the love in her own heart and the despair and disappointment in the knight's face. And as Walther, much agitated, turned away and began to pace the floor as though he could not remain quiet, Eva flung herself into her maid's arms, almost in tears.

" How," asked Magdalene, in amazement—" how could you have grown to love him, having known him for so short a time?"

" I have had his picture before me," said Eva, blushing. " Is he not like David?"

" David!" almost screamed Lene, staring at her and thinking of the 'prentice who had drawn the curtains. "Are you crazy?"

" Like David in the picture, I mean," explained Eva, smiling at the maid's mistake.

" What! Do you mean King David, with the long beard and the harp, the musician on the master's banner?"

" No!" cried Eva. " He conquering Goliath with a stone ; with sword at side, and sling in hand—the shepherd David! He who was drawn by Master Albrecht Dürer."

She clasped her hands gently, a soft light in her

eyes. Her words had started Lene upon a new line
of thought, and she now sighed, pensively, " David!
Ah, David! What misfortune you have dealt !"

The youth David had disappeared a few moments
before, and now returned, a foot-rule in his girdle,
and in his hand a string with a large piece of chalk
attached to it. " Here I am !" he announced, with
apparent pride. " Who calls me ?"

" David!" said Lene, pretending to be frightened.
" You have shut us up in here, have you not ?"

" Yes," said David, sentimentally, " and I have
shut you up in my heart !"

At this Magdalene seemed much touched. She
had long ago given her heart to the handsome young
apprentice, whose master was a near neighbor of her
own employer. As for David, he was a merry, care-
less fellow, who was very fond of Lene, and also of
the good things with which she surreptitiously pro-
vided him.

" Is there to be a frolic here ?" asked Magdalene.

" Oho ! A frolic ? No ! A very grave thing !"
declared David, with mock solemnity. " I am preparing for the masters !"

" Ah ! Is there to be singing?"

" It is merely a trial. Whoever passes the exam-
ination will be a master."

Magdalene turned excitedly to Eva. " This is
the right place for the knight !" she exclaimed.

" Come, Evchen," dropping into the affectionate speech common between them in spite of the difference in station, " we must hurry home !" Then turning to the knight, who had seen that they were about to depart, and had drawn near to escort them, she added, " If you would win our Eva's hand, Sir Knight, the time and place are favorable."

Two 'prentices entered, carrying benches, and Magdalene saw that the hour was at hand for the meeting of the guild.

" How shall I begin ? What must I do ?" exclaimed poor Walther, in great discouragement and wonder.

" David will tell you," replied Magdalene. " David, my dear friend, tell the knight all the rules. You shall have the best of the larder to-morrow if he is made a master to-day !"

Walther whispered passionately to Eva that he would see her that evening and tell her the result of his trial. Then Magdalene hurried her mistress away.

David, who had been eying the young man with a wise smile, now came forward, and said, with some derision : " A master ! Oho ! you have courage !"

The 'prentices had moved a great chair with a high step from the wall to the centre of the floor, and the knight flung himself into it, and began to think drearily of his small chances of gaining entrance to the guild.

The 'prentices now hastened in and proceeded to move benches forward in position opposite the high chair, and to prepare in every way for the meeting.

David fixed his eyes upon the face of the knight, and cried, loudly, " Now begin!"

Walther asked the meaning of this sudden command, and David told him that upon that cry, given by the master appointed marker, he must begin to sing. On learning that his hearer had never been at a song trial, that he was neither " school-man " nor " scholar," and could not say if he were either poet or singer, David was much disturbed. He talked with him in some wonder, asking several times, incredulously, if he really wished to become a master. He himself, he explained, had been apprenticed to Hans Sachs, the shoemaker, and, with great toil, was learning cobbling and singing at the same time.

He then proceeded to give a few of the rules of the Mastersingers, and the full list of the " modes " and " styles " of their songs. At the end of this recital Walther fairly gasped. " Ah !" said David, with a smile of superiority, " those are only the titles. Think of the singing !"

Indeed, the knight did think of the singing ; and he still thought of it when David, called by the 'prentices, left him, to superintend the hanging of curtains about a small platform upon which stood a desk, a seat, and a black-board.

"That is for the marker," said David, returning to his pupil. "During a song trial he marks every fault, up to seven. After that the singer is declared outdone and outsung, and pronounced incapable of becoming a master."

He stepped back hastily as the door opened and Veit Pogner and Beckmesser entered, talking together. Walther withdrew and seated himself upon one of the farthest benches.

Pogner walked with dignity, Sixtus Beckmesser with an unsteady, stealthy gait. From the top of his bald head to his mincing feet Beckmesser was a creature to be looked upon with dislike and amusement. He was born to be a clown, his own solemnity adding to his ludicrous aspect. He talked with the goldsmith in regard to his hope of winning Eva's hand in the grand song festival on the morrow.

Walther, after watching them from afar for a few moments, advanced and, much to Beckmesser's disgust, greeted Pogner, announcing his intention of trying to gain entrance to the Guild of Mastersingers. Beckmesser fairly snarled with rage at so formidable a rival, but was content with his inward conviction—that the knight, at all events, could not sing.

Nachtigall and Vogelgesang entering at the mo-

ment, Pogner introduced Walther to them, and then
to the rest of the guild, who soon entered. Before
long all the Mastersingers were assembled, and as
Kothner read forth the names from a list, each answered and seated himself.

Thereupon Pogner announced his offer of his
daughter's hand as a prize for the morrow's contest.
His words were met with applause, and when the
exclamations of approval had grown less loud he
formally presented Sir Walther von Stolzing, a
knight of Franconia—"a young man," quoth the
good Pogner, "of whom my friends have spoken
well and write as favorably. He has come to make
our Nuremberg his home, and desires to become a
disciple of that glorious art to which we all are
devoted."

"Who taught you the art of song?" was the first
question put by Kothner.

And Walther answered, " By the quiet hearth, in
winter, when castles and houses were covered with
snow, I read of the mysteries of spring in an old
book, written long ago by one of my ancestors. Sir
Walther von der Vogelweide has been my master."

"A good master!" said Hans Sachs, warmly. But
Beckmesser croaked sharply, " Long dead, however.
What could he know of our rules?"

" Then did you learn to sing in any school?"
asked Kothner.

"When the fields were free from the frost," answered Walther, dreamily, "what I learned in winter from the book I saw revealed. The spring came with marvellous, soft music. In the woods I learned my singing."

The masters were much puzzled at the boldness of a man who, without instruction in any school, yet dared to present himself as a candidate for the position of Mastersinger. Still, they consented to Hans Sachs's kindly persuasions, and informed Sir Walther von Stolzing that he should be given fair trial in the art of song.

Beckmesser was appointed marker, and, with a smile which he intended to seem sweet but which was sinister instead, the town-clerk vanished behind the curtains.

Kothner read a list of rules, none of which Walther could understand in the least, and the singer was then ordered to sit in the high chair and face the masters. This annoyed him, but he endured it for Eva's sake.

There was a pause. "The singer is ready," announced Kothner.

"Now begin!" cried Beckmesser, the marker, from behind the curtains.

Walther could not tell what inspired him, but he no longer asked himself what he should sing. Words and notes flowed swiftly and simply from his heart:

"Now begin!
So calls the spring through the trees,
And wakens harmonies;
From forests tones are welling,
    And thence float far and clear,
Then comes a mighty swelling
    Of melody drawn near.
The wood around is filled with sound
From tender voices ringing,
And clear and loud the echoes crowd,
Song grows and swells like pealing bells,
Exultant is the singing!
The wood with flood of answer meets the cry,
Life wakes to love—and high
Sounds anew the joyous song of spring!"

A diligent scratching could be heard behind the
curtain, and weary sighs from the marker.   Walther
changed his song:

"In thorny thicket hiding,
    His heart grown cold with hate,
Grim winter is presiding
    Alone and desolate.
The dead leaves rustle where
He lurks and listens there;
He would the happy singing
To sorrow black be bringing!"

Walther rose excitedly at this point of his song
and sang the second verse.   In exquisite words and
stirring music he compared the love in his own heart

to the awakening spring; but, as he paused at the end of a stanza, Beckmesser rushed out from between the curtains, showing the black-board, which he had completely covered with chalk-marks indicating Walther's errors.

The masters laughed heartily at this, and at Beckmesser's frantic joy at the failure of the knight. After talking it over, they decided that Sir Walther would better sing no more, as he was already out-sung, according to the rules of the guild. Hans Sachs alone had been touched by the beauty of what Walther had sung, and bade the masters have patience, saying that though it was not composed or rendered in observance of their rules, it yet seemed well worth hearing, and he concluded by beseeching Walther to finish his song. In spite of jeers from Beckmesser and exclamations of disapprobation from the masters, the knight obeyed, thereby winning the good cobbler's admiration by his perseverance in the face of such discouragement.

Beckmesser capered with mingled triumph and fury; the masters all talked at once; the 'prentices, who had hitherto remained apart, now jumped up and danced gayly, much enjoying the confusion— still Walther sang on, and Hans Sachs strained his ears to hear above the tumult the music which filled his poetical heart with delight.

At last the Mastersingers raised their hands, the signal for silence.

" Now, masters," cried Beckmesser, "give your decision !"

The masters spoke in unison, and with great impressiveness :

" Outdone and outsung !"

Walther stopped abruptly, bowed to the masters with a look of combined pride and contempt, and hastily left the church. The Mastersingers also departed, for the guild meeting was over.

Hans Sachs stood looking musingly on the great empty chair, and the memory of the Song of Spring came over him. Then he turned away and followed the other masters, having suddenly remembered that he was an ignorant old cobbler, who was incapable of understanding such genius, and who must forget it and return to his work.

Leading Melodies of the Song of Spring

(Used also as the Love Motif)

Cobbling Motif

CHAPTER II

HANS SACHS, THE COBBLER

VEIT POGNER and Hans Sachs lived opposite
each other in corner houses, with a broad street run-
ning in one direction, and a narrow and crooked alley in the other. Pogner's house was large and pre-
tentious, with a high flight of steps, and a linden-
tree which spread its branches over a comfortable
garden-seat. Hans Sachs's cottage was small, and
his workshop opened out onto a little plot of grass
with a shady elder-tree.

It was twilight on the day, which, though its real
title was St. John's Eve, was called Midsummer
Eve, and Folly-tide as well. Afternoon had given
place to the cool, quiet dusk. The 'prentices were
frolicking in the old street, singing and jesting. They

were performing their evening duties and closing the shutters on the lower floors of their masters' houses.

Magdalene came out from Pogner's door and called David, showing him the tempting contents of a basket which she carried.

" How went it with the knight?" she asked, in a whisper.

When David replied that he had been declared outdone and outsung, the maid returned to the house in great perturbation, the meaning of which David could not fathom, and with the basket still on her arm, a fact which caused him deep disappointment. The 'prentices shouted with mockery at his discomfiture, and David, feeling obliged to be angry with some one, began to fight the merry boys who had surrounded him, and were dancing and capering while they derided him.

Meanwhile a figure had appeared in the alley, and now advanced with slow tread ; the figure of a tall, strong man in rough coat and stout boots, with a full beard, ruddy cheeks, and honest eyes. It was Hans Sachs, the cobbler. He parted the boys, suggesting that they all go to bed, which advice was rapidly followed by the 'prentices, who were some-what confused at having shown such foolishness before Hans Sachs. David was ordered to do some cobbling before retiring, and he and his master entered the house together.

Pogner and Eva came slowly through the alley, having been walking in the fresh evening air. Seating themselves under the linden-tree, the father and daughter talked for a few moments, and Eva tried gently to persuade him to say that he who might aspire to her hand need not be a Mastersinger. Pogner was firm, but something in her voice aroused new thoughts in his brain. He wondered if the knight who had failed in the song trial had been in his daughter's mind while she spoke. When Eva reminded him that their supper was ready he arose, and walked musingly into the house.

Magdalene had hastened to meet Eva, and now whispered to her the information about Walther imparted by David.

" How can I find out about it?" exclaimed Eva, in distress.

" Hans Sachs," suggested Magdalene, doubtfully.

" Ah ! He is fond of me, I know. Yes, I will go to him !" And Eva smiled, much relieved. Magdalene told her not to go until after supper, that her father might not suspect her errand. Then both hastened within.

Sachs, having removed his coat, came to the door of his house ready for work. He bade David bring him his stool and cobbling-bench and then go to bed.

" Why will you work by this bad light?" asked the 'prentice, as he obeyed.

"You need not wait," was all Sachs's answer.

"Sleep well, master," said David, and turned away.

"Good-night!" returned Sachs, arranging his tools before him.

His door was divided into upper and lower halves, swinging separately. The upper part was open, and he leaned upon the lower half, looking out into the quiet street, feeling the cool wind against his face and breathing the sweet odor blown from the elder-tree. For the time his work was forgotten and he sat motionless, content to see and feel so much loveliness.

"The fragrance from the elder-tree makes me long for words," he murmured, dreamily. Then he added abruptly, after a deep sigh, "Of what account are my thoughts? I am but a poor, stupid man! Poetry is a pleasure when my work grows too detestable, but I would better let it go and keep to my leather."

He caught up one of the shoes on the bench before him, and began to hammer it noisily. For some time he worked; then, suddenly, like a faint, beautiful echo, the melody of the Song of Spring drifted through his mind; he paused, and leaned back, trying to catch the elusive memory. He could not quite remember it, but he knew that the very thought of it brought dreams of innumerable birdsongs in May, of things old yet seeming new, so strangely sweet had been the singing.

He was still musing on the knight and his song when Eva crossed the street from Pogner's house to his.

"Good-evening, master!" she said—"still at work?"

" Hey, Evchen, dear !" exclaimed Sachs, delightedly. " Have you come to speak of the shoes I made for you to wear at the festival to-morrow ?"

Eva answered that they were so fine that as yet she had not even tried them on, and seated herself beside him. After a short talk, during which Eva seemed in one of her gay, mocking moods, and Sachs spoke with an undercurrent of tenderness and sadness, she began to question him in regard to the guild meeting that morning.

Sachs said that a knight had attempted to become one of the guild, but had been voted outsung by the masters.

The cobbler suspected that there was some hidden reason for the interest which Eva evinced for the unfortunate knight, and, in order to decide this definitely, he pretended to have been ill-pleased with him, and spoke with much disapproval of his song.

Eva, fairly furious at this, rose and, in response to a summons from Magdalene, hurried across the street, flinging a few parting words of reproach to

11

Sachs: "You use pitch for your shoemaking; you would much better light a fire with it and try to warm your cold, unkind soul!"

Hans Sachs looked after her, nodding with a wise and tender smile.

"That is what I thought," he said to himself, and gathering up his working materials, he entered the house.

"Your father called you," whispered Magdalene, as Eva joined her at Pogner's door. "But wait— before you go in hear this: I met Master Sixtus Beckmesser, who told me that he was coming to-night to serenade you with the same song with which he hopes to win you to-morrow."

"You must take my place," declared Eva, "and listen to his song. I must wait for my knight, for he told me he would come this evening."

Pogner's voice was heard calling, "Lene! Eva!" and Magdalene attempted to draw her mistress within the door, but at that moment Walther appeared, hastening up the narrow alley, and Eva flew to meet him. So all that Magdalene could do was to beseech her not to stay long. She then entered the house, leaving the knight and her mistress together.

Walther soon told Eva the story of his rejection by the guild, and described the narrowness and stupidity of the miserable masters, who, he de-

"SHE BEGAN TO QUESTION HIM IN REGARD TO THE GUILD MEETING"

clared, had derided his Song of Spring and cruelly scoffed at his tribute to love.

He grew more and more enraged as he continued, and finally succeeded in working himself up to a veritable frenzy at his recollections of that terrible song trial. The long-drawn note of an ox-horn in the distance made him start and clasp the hilt of his sword.

" It is only the watchman," explained Eva, soothingly. " Come and hide under the linden-tree."

The old watchman appeared, carrying a lantern and singing his evening exhortation to peaceable customs:

> " To my words ye people hearken:
> Your houses straightway darken!
> 'Tis ten o'clock, all fires put out!
> Let naught of evil lurk about.
> Praise give to the Lord!"

With a long blast on his ox-horn he departed. Hans Sachs, within his house, had heard through his half-open door whispered words from Walther and Eva—words which told him that they were planning to go away together and be married, since Pogner would only give his daughter to a follower of art, and Walther could never be a Mastersinger. The cobbler opened wide his door and looked out. A few minutes before he did so Eva had gone into

the house, and now crept out in Magdalene's dress,
having changed costumes with the maid. She hastened to Walther's side, and Hans Sachs relapsed
into thought.

He decided that they must not be allowed to
elope; but, he further concluded, it would be most
unjust to keep them apart; they must be allowed
to wed — that was certain — and he made up his
mind to bring this about.

He first turned his lamp so that a broad stream
of light fell through the doorway across the street.
Walther and Eva would have to pass through this
belt of brightness before they could escape, and this
he knew they would not wish to do, lest they should
be seen.

The cobbler was unexpectedly aided in his plans
by Beckmesser, who arrived with his lute to serenade Eva. When they saw the approaching minstrel, the lovers drew swiftly back into the foliage.

Walther was hurt and wounded by his merciless
defeat, and reckless enough to forget Eva's real
welfare in his desire to carry her away from the terrible masters. Eva, who was little more than an in-
experienced child, did not think of her father, whom
she was deciding to leave, nor of her home. Thinking of nothing save her love and the happiness for
which she hoped, she had contentedly agreed to go
away with her knight from Nuremberg.

Sachs quietly carried his work-bench and lamp outside his door and seated himself. Beckmesser tuned his lute vigorously, practising various passages and chords. Suddenly Sachs lifted his hammer, struck a sharp blow upon one of the shoes which he held, and, having greatly startled Beckmesser, proceeded to sing a loud cobbling-song.

Beckmesser tried to silence him, but Sachs explained that he was making the town-clerk's own shoes, and that he always sang while at work. He then went on with his song once more. Beckmesser was particularly disturbed by the thought that Eva might possibly mistake Hans Sachs's voice for his. Finally, much agitated, he began to pace up and down, his hands at his ears, to shut out the sound of the cobbling-song.

Sachs, as he worked and sang, drifted from the boisterous humor of the first stanzas into words of tenderer and deeper meaning. He sang to the Angel of Poetry, his consoler and helper:

> " Oh ! hearken to my cry of woe,
>   My heavy, sad vexation:
> Those works of art shoemakers show
>   Receive small approbation!
> If to my toil and grief
> No angel brought relief,
> And called me oft to Paradise,
> I'd leave these shoes that I despise!

But when he lifts me heavenward,
The world beneath me I discard;
    Rest comes unto
    Hans Sachs, the shoe-
    Maker and the poet too!"

"Ah," whispered Eva, feeling a strange pain in her heart; "the song brings me grief—I know not why."

One of the shutters on Pogner's house opened, and Magdalene, in Eva's dress, appeared.

Beckmesser prepared for his serenade. He sought to silence and propitiate Sachs by asking him to listen to his song and to give him his critical opinion, worth so much in Nuremberg. But Sachs would not listen, and began to repeat the first part of his cobbling-song. Beckmesser urged that he would wake the neighbors with his noise, but Sachs replied that they were used to it, and would pay no attention.

At last he consented to hear the song if he might mark each error by a tap of his hammer upon one of the shoes which he was making. In this way he hoped to get well on with his work before the end of the serenade.

Beckmesser reluctantly agreed to this, and began to sing to Magdalene, the supposed Eva, accompanying himself upon his lute. A very ridiculous and unmusical performance it was, and Sachs found

so many grave faults against time and tune that he
was kept busy tapping, and by the end of the song
had finished both shoes.

The loud sounds had at last awakened the neighbors; windows began to open, and nightcaps to ap-
pear. The men, seeing that there was some disturbance in the street below, soon arrived on the scene,
and the clamor grew and swelled.

David, startled by the general tumult, opened his
window on the ground-floor of Sachs's cottage. Seeing Beckmesser singing to a woman, whom the 'prentice recognized to be Magdalene, he became extremely jealous, and, providing himself with a cud-
gel, leaped out of the window and began to belabor
the unfortunate musician.

The excitement increased, though no one knew
the real cause or beginning of the commotion. Finally, as such disturbances often end, there was a
general street fight, and masters, apprentices, and
ordinary burghers beat each other unmercifully.

Walther and Eva tried to push through the crowd
and escape in the general confusion to the city gate,
where the knight's servants and horses waited. But
divining their purpose, Sachs started forward and
grasped Walther's arm, pushing Eva towards her
father, who had appeared on the steps of his house,
crying, " Lene !" and now caught her hand, thinking
her the maid, and drew her within.

Sachs fairly dragged the knight into his workshop and shut the door. David released Beckmesser, and at that instant the sound of the ox-horn was heard in the distance. The people hastily dispersed. In a very few moments the street was empty and quiet.

The sleepy old watchman came, rubbing his eyes and yawning, and wondering if he could have dreamed that he heard a noise. Much puzzled, he shook his head, peered down the alley, and repeated his call commanding all good people to be at peace. Then, blowing his ox-horn, he walked slowly on once more.

The full moon rose above the roofs at this moment, the air was sweet and cool, the houses were dark. Rest seemed to lie like a cloak upon the old city of Nuremberg. The watchman paused at the corner, fancying that he heard a sound, but all was silent, and, turning, he went on his way down the moonlit street.

Hans Sachs's Cobbling-Song

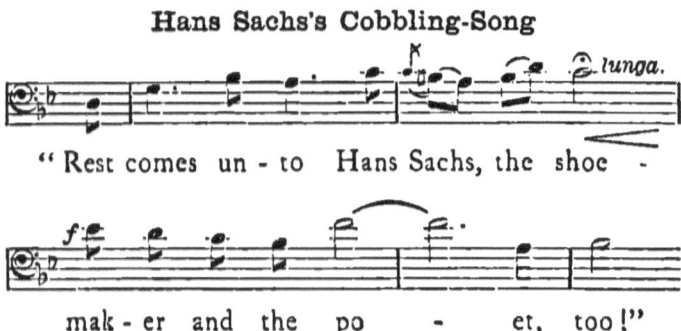

" Rest comes un - to Hans Sachs, the shoe -

mak - er and the po - et, too!"

Motif of David

CHAPTER III

THE COBBLER'S WORKSHOP

IT was St. John's Day. The morning sunshine fell brightly into Hans Sachs's workshop and upon his bent head as he sat near the window reading an old folio with dusty covers and yellow pages.

So absorbed was he that he did not hear David enter the house. The prentice carried a basket upon his arm which he proceeded to open. Inside it were flowers and gay ribbons, and at the bottom a superb sausage and a deliciously tempting cake. He had begun to eye these dainties with the intention of eating them at once, when Sachs turned over a leaf of his folio with a suddenness which startled David.

Thinking that his master had summoned him, he advanced to his side, assuring him that he had carried the shoes to Master Beckmesser, as directed; and, finally, as Sachs was silent, he asked his pardon for his misdeeds of the previous night. He explained that he had been jealous of Beckmesser because Lene had been very cold to him in the afternoon, and he had been on the lookout for the cause of her displeasure.

"But now Lene is kind again," he added, "and, for the festival, has given me these flowers and ribbons."

Sachs had paid no attention to his words, but he now closed the book and gazed past the 'prentice towards the articles which David had taken from the basket.

"Flowers and ribbons do I see there?" he said, softly. "They seem like the fancies of youth. How came they into my house?"

David reminded him that it was the feast day of St. John, and that every one must be gay.

"Ah, yes! Last night was your Folly Eve," said Sachs, musingly.

After a few moments, during which David wondered if he were very angry, Sachs told him to sing him the Song of St. John, which he had learned. The boy obeyed, first, by mistake, singing the words to the air of Beckmesser's serenade. He hastily corrected himself, with a laugh, and sang the song through. Having finished, he offered the sausage which Lene had given him to his master.

"Thank you, my lad," said Sachs, quietly. "Keep it for yourself, and deck yourself with the flowers

"READING AN OLD FOLIO WITH DUSTY COVERS"

and the ribbons for the festival. You shall go before me like my herald."

" Ah, master !" cried honest David, with tears in his eyes. "I should like better to be your groomsman ! Why should you not wed again ? Beckmesser cannot win," he added, confidentially.

" That may well be," answered Sachs, smiling ; and then said, gently, " Go now, and array yourself gayly. And be careful not to wake Sir Walther."

David obeyed, and the cobbler was left alone. He gazed down at the book lying on his knees, but he did not read. Instead, he fell into a deep reverie. He seemed to see the world before him, full of striving people ; and the memory of the Folly Eve twisted itself into fantastical, symbolic shape.

First he pictured Nuremberg sleeping, content with old rules and old customs; then, through a shoemaker, a commotion arose—madness seemed to be in every one. " Let us see what Hans Sachs can do," he murmured, " to make the madness serve for noble ends."

A door opened, and Walther appeared on the threshold of Sachs's room.

As he saw him the cobbler rose, letting his book slide unnoticed to the floor.

" Good greeting, Sir Knight ! You were awake late ; but did you finally have rest?"

" What sleep I had was very sound and good,"

replied Walther, advancing. He seemed dreamy
and preoccupied, and when the shoemaker again
addressed him, the young man exclaimed, with a
rapt look, " I had a marvellously lovely dream !"

" That is good !" said his host, kindly. " Relate
it to me."

" I fear to put it into words," declared Walther,
softly.

" My friend," said Sachs—and there was much
wisdom and sweetness in the smile which came to
his lips—" the poet's work is to put dreams into
words. In dreams men's highest thoughts come to
them, and poetry is only dreaming made real."
Then he added, humorously, " Did your dream tell
you how you might become a master?"

" No," said Walther, quietly, but with suppressed
bitterness. " No; the masters had no place in my
dream !"

" But," persisted Sachs, " did it teach you no
magic by which you might conquer?"

" How can you hope longer?" asked the knight,
quickly and despairingly.

" Indeed, my hope has far from left me," said
Sachs; and added, jokingly, " if it had, I should
have run away with you last night, instead of with-
holding you !" He paused a moment; then, with
great kindliness in his eyes and voice, he continued:
" Remember that in the masters you have to deal

with honorable men. In spite of their mistakes,
you must accept them as they are. Judges and
donors of a prize must consider a song justly, according to their convictions, and they could not approve of yours, because it was fashioned at variance
with their rules—rules made by old, worn men, as
a means of framing music to remind them of their
lost spring-time. These rules are worth considering, and if you will but follow them, and yet give
your idea full scope, you must make a mastersong.
Take for your subject your morning dream and try
now."

" But one is a dream, and one should be poetry,"
began Walther, perplexed.

" They are friends," said Sachs, smiling. " Now,
sing the description of your dream. I will correct
you if you make errors."

He drew towards him a piece of paper and a pen,
and wrote down the words of the knight as, after a
moment's pause, he began to sing :

> " Morning light brightened with roseate beam;
> Flower fragrance rare
> Swelled through the air;
> My eyes with rapture then did capture
> A garden all a-gleam—
> Such was my dream !"

" That," said Sachs, as he wrote, " is a stanza.

Now be sure that the next is like it, and, in form,
wedded to the first."

" Why?" asked the knight.

" That people may know you are going to be
married!" said Sachs, his eyes twinkling with fun.
Walther laughed, and continued :

> " Wondrous above that bright garden, alone,
> A fragrant tree
> Stood royally,
> It's fair boughs showing the fruits there growing,
> Gold fruitage richly grown,
> 'Mid scents soft-blown."

Sachs smiled delightedly, then shook his head.
" You close in a different key from the beginning ;
the masters do not like that ; but I agree with you
—it is always so in spring.   Now sing the After-
song."

Walther sang once more :

> " Hear while I tell
> What marvel awed me, gazing there :
> A woman met my wondering sight—
> Ne'er saw I one so sweet, so fair !
> Heed what befell—
> I clasped her, in supreme delight ;
> With soft eyes glowing,
> She pointed—showing
> What roused desires manifold :
> The fruit that crowned with gold
> The Tree of Life !"

" That is really an After-song!" said Sachs, much
touched. " The verse is complete; but with the
melody you are a trifle free. I do not say that I
dislike it; but 'tis not easy to remember, and that
annoys our old masters."

He then bade Walther sing a second verse. The
knight obeyed, making his theme and climax the
Tree of Fame, instead of the Tree of Life.

Having finished it, he declared that he had completed the narrative of his dream, and had no more
to sing. After entreating him not to forget the
melody, Sachs said that the knight's servant had
arrived some time before—" With the clothes in
which I suppose you had expected to be married,"
added the cobbler. "A bird must have pointed out
the way to his master! Come, now, and don all the
finery for the festival." He led the way to the
door of his room, paused respectfully for Walther
to pass through, and followed him.

No sooner had the door closed than Sixtus Beckmesser entered the workshop from the street, limp-
ing painfully, for he had not yet recovered from the
effects of David's cudgelling. So intense was his
nervousness that he paused and stared about him at
every step—ran, then stumbled; wheeled about to
return to the door, then hastily advanced. At last
he reached the chair wherein the cobbler had med-
itated so deeply, and stood looking down at the

table. There he saw a slip of paper which, with his customary inquisitiveness, he lifted. He glanced through it, and seeing that it was a love-song in Hans Sachs's writing, he instantly concluded that the cobbler was going to compete for the master-prize.

He had only time to put the paper into his pocket when Sachs, in festival garb, entered the workshop, and greeted the town-clerk with much surprise, asking if the shoes sent him that morning were unsatisfactory.

Beckmesser declared, angrily, that the shoes were miserable things, thin and ill-fitting. He then burst into a storm of fury, telling Sachs that he now knew the depth of his cunning, and accusing him of dishonesty in pretending to be disinterested and devoted to art when he himself was really a suitor for Eva's hand, and an aspirant for the laurel-wreath of victory.

These suppositions Sachs quietly denied.

" But I hold proof!" persisted Beckmesser, searching in his pocket. The cobbler glanced at the table and saw that the song-poem was gone.

" Is this your writing?" demanded the town-clerk, showing the paper which he had taken from his pocket.

" Yes," replied Sachs. " Of what matter is that?"

" Is the writing fresh?" continued Beckmesser, shaking with rage.

Sachs nodded. " And the ink is still wet," he said.

" Is it a love-song ?" screamed the clerk, wrathful, but triumphant.

" Undoubtedly," answered Sachs, much amused.

" Well!" cried Beckmesser, breathlessly.

" Well, what more ?"

" You ask that ?" gasped the town-clerk.

" Why not ask it ?" tranquilly responded Sachs.

" Then," declared Beckmesser, "you must be the blackest knave alive !"

" Perhaps," said the cobbler, quietly ; " but still I think I have never put papers belonging to another in my own pocket. That you may not be considered a thief, I give you leave to keep the song."

Now the song was one such as the town-clerk would wish to sing before the judges, and the gift filled him with so much amazement and rapture that it was long before he could collect his wits. Finally he recovered sufficiently to beseech Sachs to promise that he would never tell any one that the song was composed by him. This touched the cobbler's sense of humor, but he controlled his amusement and answered, " No one shall ever be told by me that that song is mine !"

Wild with delight, Beckmesser embraced him

12

gratefully, and danced to the door. Suddenly fancying in his excitement that he had left the paper on
the table, he flew back to look. When he saw it in
his own hand, he once more embraced the cobbler,
and gayly leaped, limped, and capered to the door
of the workshop and down the street.

A smile came to Sachs's lips as he watched him
depart, and he murmured to himself: "So much
evil in one man I have never before found. He will
be punished some day."

The good cobbler had given the song to his late
visitor with his eyes well open. He knew that Beckmesser could not find a melody which would fit the
poetry, even if he could remember the words; and
though, being above petty trickery, he had not deceived the town-clerk, he yet felt that Beckmesser,
by his foolishness and conceit, would ruin his own
opportunities, and that Walther's would thereby be
bettered.

Looking up, suddenly, Sachs saw Eva, in a holiday
dress of white, standing at the door of the workshop,
and started forward, exclaiming, "Greeting, my
Evchen! Hey! how fine you are to-day!"

Eva's face was pale and her eyes were sad. She
seemed troubled and vexed. Declaring that her
shoe hurt her, she advanced to a stool which Sachs
brought, and put her foot upon it. First she said
that it was too tight, then assured him that it was

"'AHA! NOW I HAVE FOUND THE PLACE THAT HURTS'"

far too wide. Finally she indicated the various parts of her foot which were hurt by the ill-fitting shoe.

As Sachs knelt, trying to discover the fault, Walther opened the chamber door and came in, dressed in the rich garb of a knight. Eva uttered a cry, and Sachs said, softly, "Aha ! Now I have found the place that hurts ! Wait, and I will fix it."

He gently removed her shoe, while she stood motionless, her foot upon the stool, and went to his bench. He began to work upon the shoe, pretending not to notice Walther, who still stood at the door of the inner room, gazing at Eva.

"Always cobbling!" said Sachs, as he worked. "That is my fate both night and day. Once upon a time, I thought of ending this shoemaking by entering the contest; then I might become a poet. It was certainly you, child, who made me think of that ! But—well, you are right ! I seem to hear you say —'Go on, and make your shoes !' However, will no one else sing ? I heard a lovely song to-day. I wonder if a third verse might not be forthcoming ?"

Gazing on the face of the maiden before him, Walther began to sing. He sang of the starlight which shone from the eyes of the beautiful woman in the garden, and her marvellous tenderness, which waked the sleeping poet within his heart, and blessed him with the glory of the Dream of Love.

As he sang, Sachs continued to work quietly at
the shoe. Finally he brought it to Eva, and gently
put it on her foot once more. When Walther began to sing the cobbler had said, " Hark, child ; this
is a Mastersong!" And, as the tender melody came
to a close, he whispered, softly, " Was I not right ?
Try the shoe now : does it still hurt ?"

Eva burst into a storm of sobs and sank into
Sachs's arms, clinging to him and weeping passionately. Walther advanced and grasped the cobbler's
hand silently, unable to speak. Sachs himself was
deeply moved with both sadness and happiness.
After a moment or two he put Eva gently from him
and turned away, talking loudly and jovially, leaving
them standing together.

A few minutes passed, and then Eva came towards him, her face bright with smiles and tears.

" You are my best and truest friend," she said,
brokenly ; " without you, what should I be ?—a
child, weak and blind. Through you I feel that I
am awake and living and a woman. I feel my own
soul for the first time—and all through you."

Sachs would scarcely listen to her words of gratitude. At this point Magdalene, gayly dressed, appeared at the shop door, and David came out from
his room, decked out with the flowers and ribbons.
Sachs bade them all gather around, and told them
that they must witness the christening of a Master-

song. "David, as a 'prentice, cannot be witness," said the cobbler; "so I will set him free from his apprenticeship and make him a journeyman."

David knelt, and received a box on the ear from Sachs and a few words declaring his freedom.

Then, with great solemnity, the shoemaker said that the song should be called the "Glorious Song of the Morning Dream," and requested Eva, whom he laughingly appointed godmother, to say a few words suited to the occasion.

Eva's voice trembled as she spoke, describing the tender beauty of the song, and all echoed her simple words. Meanwhile, Magdalene and David whispered together. Walther seemed overpowered by his happiness, and the cobbler smiled upon them all with tears in his eyes.

After the wonder and delight of all had somewhat abated, Sachs told Eva and Magdalene to go to Pogner, who was waiting for them. They hastily obeyed, and the cobbler and knight, with the new-made journeyman, left the shop and made their way to the scene of the coming festival.

Sachs's Reverie

CHAPTER IV

THE SINGING OF THE MASTERSONG

SOME miles from Nuremberg, where the river Pegnitz wound its way between the meadows, the people assembled for the festival. A raised platform, with benches and seats upon it, was ready for the masters. Under gayly colored tents people were partaking of refreshments of all sorts.

Companies composed of members of different trades soon arrived — the cobblers, the tailors, the bakers, the watchmen, the lute-makers, the journeymen, and all the busy workpeople of Nuremberg. Trumpets and horns sounded, and loud sounds of gayety filled the air.

The 'prentices, dressed in extravagantly gaudy costumes trimmed with ribbons, rushed about, acting as ushers and ordering the tradespeople around. They all ran to the water's edge as a boat hung with bright flags arrived at the landing, filled with young peasant girls in festival dresses.

" Maidens from Fürth! Maidens from Fürth!" cried the 'prentices. " Town-piper, play !"

They helped the girls out of the boat and began to dance about with them, eluding the journeymen, who would have liked to have danced themselves.

David arrived at this point, and looked disapprovingly on the merrymaking.

" Dancing, are you !" he commented, disgustedly. " What would the masters say ?"

The 'prentices did not answer, and only made faces at him. At this David cried, " I might as well have a good time, too !" and seizing the hands of a pretty peasant girl standing near, joined in the dance with much fervor. After a time the 'prentices shouted, " The Mastersingers! The Mastersingers !" and the dance came to a hasty end.

The 'prentices formed a line, the people parted, and the Mastersingers, in a slow and stately procession, made their way to the platform, Kothner preceeding them, and bearing a banner upon which was a design representing David the King, with his harp. The people cheered them loudly, and waved their hats and scarfs in great excitement. Pogner led Eva, who was followed by a troop of maidens, to her place on the platform. The masters seated themselves on the long benches prepared for them ;

the journeymen stood behind, and the apprentices advanced towards the people, crying, " Silentium !"

Sachs rose from his place, and at sight of him all the people doffed their hats and caps, pointing and whispering, and finally broke out into a grand chorus, which they had learned for the occasion, hailing the nightingale which sang so sweetly in the dawn.

" Hail !" they ended, pointing towards the embarrassed cobbler—" Hail to Nuremberg's beloved Hans Sachs !"

Sachs answered their tribute in words of humility, dignity, and gratitude ; and then formally announced Pogner's gift of his daughter in marriage as the prize that day.

" Masters," he added—" all who to-day compete in the trial of song—think what a prize is here, and be sure that he who would win such a crown of art has a heart full of simple love, nobility, and poetry ! So will the Mastersingers be worthy the honor of Nuremberg."

While the applause which met his speech still continued, he turned to Beckmesser, who was trying vainly to learn the song by heart, and accosted him in low tones, kindly advising him to give up all idea of singing it. But the town-clerk was determined, and when Kothner bade all bachelor masters prepare for the contest, and called on Beckmesser, as the oldest, to come forward, he took his lute and was conducted by the 'prentices to a mound of turf which they had erected and strewn with flowers.

When he insisted that it was too rickety they laughed under their breath, and hammered the mound with their spades. The people near Beckmesser began to joke and whisper together about his unprepossessing appearance, and, feeling very hot, nervous, and uncertain of himself, the minstrel mounted the mound and balanced himself there, waiting for the signal.

" Now begin !" cried Kothner, and Beckmesser, having bowed to the masters, the people, and Eva —who turned away in displeasure—played a tuneless prelude on his lute and began to sing.

Not one word of the song which Sachs had given him could he remember ; even the sense vanished away in the extreme confusion of his brain ; the melody was much like that of his unlucky serenade, and, altogether, so strange a song had never been heard by either the masters or the people. They muttered together, stared, laughed, and finally relinquished all attempt at comprehension, and listened to the unmusical and apparently senseless performance to the end.

At the last words, Beckmesser, infuriated by the loud laughter which met the conclusion of his song, sprang towards Sachs, flung the paper at his feet and, shouting that it was Sachs who had written the poetry and, consequently, Sachs who must be blamed for its foolishness, rushed away and disappeared in the crowd.

Much amazed, the masters asked Sachs to explain this astounding assertion, and the cobbler answered that Beckmesser had made a mistake, that he had not written the song, and indeed could never hope to compose anything so fine. As the masters were still incredulous that there could be anything save nonsense in the composition, Sachs said that Beckmesser had undoubtedly sung it incorrectly, and that they would appreciate its beauty if it were properly rendered and set to a better melody. Any one who could successfully sing the verses, Sachs declared, would prove not only that he himself was their author, but that he was worthy a place among the masters.

"Will no one come forward?" he called. "Is there not one who will prove that I am right? If so, let him approach!"

Walther emerged from the midst of the crowd, and advanced towards the platform. As he bowed courteously to Sachs, the assembled masters, and the people, every one was pleased, and the masters, exclaiming that the cobbler had chosen a clever way of gaining his ends, consented to hear his witness's rendering of this remarkable song.

"Sir Walther von Stolzing," said Sachs, impres-

"EVA CROWNED THE VICTOR WITH A WREATH OF LAUREL AND MYRTLE."

sively, "sing this song! You, masters, pay heed to his errors."

He handed the paper to Kothner, and drew back. Walther advanced to the mound and sprang upon it. After a moment's pause he began to sing the Song of the Dream. Then, as after the first few bars the master dropped the paper and listened eagerly, he let his fancy and his passion have full poetical sway. He no longer followed the words of the song as he had composed it first; he sang new and beautiful thoughts to music such as the masters had never heard before. As he ended the first stanza, they whispered their approbation softly to one another.

"Witness in place, sing on!" called Sachs.

Again Walther sang. As though carried away on mighty waters, he sang with more and more fervor until, at the end of the second stanza, the masters could only whisper their admiration brokenly and delightedly.

"Witness, well sung!" said Sachs. "Sing on, and end!"

And with his soul thrilling to his words, Walther sent all his spirit out into the glorious melody of the Aftersong. The people, listening, broke into soft words of wonder, their hushed whispers accompanying the closing bars of this song, which had caused so strange and marvellous a joy to spring up in the masters' hearts, a joy higher and grander than all their past pride and pleasure in their art.

For the Mastersong had been sung. Masters and people cried out, proclaiming the fact, and, as though in a dream, Eva crowned the victor with a wreath of laurel and myrtle.

Pogner then came forward with a gold chain and medallion, bearing the portrait of King David, and formally admitted the knight to the guild. But Walther, remembering all his past agony and humiliation, refused to become a master, and every one, sorely disturbed and perplexed, turned as usual to Hans Sachs to right the difficulty.

The cobbler went to the young knight's side and grasped his hand. Then he spoke, kindly and gravely, and Walther, as he listened, forgot his bitterness and painful memories.

" Do not disparage the masters, but honor their art. They give you their highest praise ; not because of your name, your wealth, your high rank, or your prowess in battle, but because you are a poet, and have gained fairly the title of master. Think on these things with gratitude. And how can you dispraise the art which has bestowed upon you such a prize as yours ? Honor the German masters ; so you will banish evil. For while they live and work —though the great Roman Empire should go up in smoke—yet will remain our holy German art !"

As his last words were echoed by one and all, Eva lifted the wreath from Walther's head and placed it upon that of Sachs; and Sachs, taking the chain from Pogner, hung it around the knight's neck, and thus made him a Mastersinger of Nuremberg. The cobbler embraced the two, and while Pogner knelt as though in homage before his friend, Walther and Eva remained on either side of him, resting against him in deep love and trust.

Men waved their hats and women their kerchiefs, the 'prentices danced and clapped their hands in wild excitement, and then, while the trumpet sounded, there came a loud cry straight from the hearts of the honest, loving people of Nuremberg: " Hail, Sachs! Nuremberg's beloved Sachs!"

The Mastersong

THE END

www.ingramcontent.com/pod-product-compliance
Lightning Source LLC
Chambersburg PA
CBHW020116030726
47498CB00006B/2125